'Luc...ng down at he...yes as she scrubbed the floor of the club. 'Are you working here?'

Of course she should have said, *What's it to you?* But a row might draw attention, and she couldn't afford to lose this job.

'No, of course I'm not working here,' she protested with a laugh, glancing around to make sure no one had heard Luke calling her by her real name. 'I come here so often they let me hang my coat in the stockroom.'

'Really?' Luke drawled, with an even more contemptuous expression in his brooding amber gaze.

'Okay, I work here from time to time,' she admitted, brushing it off as she continued to stare at a face that was mesmerising in its harsh masculine beauty. If you wanted hard there was no better hard to be had than Luke Forster—as her yearning and thoroughly confused body could now attest.

The crowd on the dance floor fell back at Luke's advance like the Red Sea parting, and Luke paused at the entrance to the casino just long enough to shoot a stare at Lucia that assured her this wasn't nearly over yet.

Susan Stephens was a professional singer before meeting her husband on the tiny Mediterranean island of Malta. In true Modern™ Romance style they met on Monday, became engaged on Friday, and were married three months after that. Almost thirty years and three children later, they are still in love. (Susan does not advise her children to return home one day with a similar story, as she may not take the news with the same fortitude as her own mother!)

Susan had written several non-fiction books when fate took a hand. At a charity costume ball there was an after-dinner auction. One of the lots, 'Spend a Day with an Author', had been donated by Mills & Boon® author Penny Jordan. Susan's husband bought this lot, and Penny was to become not just a great friend but a wonderful mentor, who encouraged Susan to write romance.

Susan loves her family, her pets, her friends and her writing. She enjoys entertaining, travel, and going to the theatre. She reads, cooks, and plays the piano to relax, and can occasionally be found throwing herself off mountains on a pair of skis or galloping through the countryside. Visit Susan's website: www.susanstephens.net She loves to hear from her readers all around the world!

Recent titles by the same author:

A TASTE OF THE UNTAMED
THE ARGENTINIAN'S SOLACE
THE SHAMELESS LIFE OF RUIZ ACOSTA
THE UNTAMED ARGENTINIAN

To find out more about the wild Acosta family visit:
http://www.susanstephens.com/acostas/index.html

Did you know these are also available as eBooks?
Visit www.millsandboon.co.uk

THE MAN FROM HER WAYWARD PAST

BY
SUSAN STEPHENS

MILLS & BOON®

First published in Great Britain 2012
by Mills & Boon, an imprint of Harlequin (UK) Limited.
Harlequin (UK) Limited, Eton House, 18-24 Paradise Road,
Richmond, Surrey TW9 1SR

© Susan Stephens 2012

ISBN: 978 0 263 89335 9

Harlequin (UK) policy is to use papers that are natural, renewable
and recyclable products and made from wood grown in sustainable
forests. The logging and manufacturing process conform to the
legal environmental regulations of the country of origin.

Printed and bound in Spain
by Blackprint CPI, Barcelona

THE MAN
FROM HER
WAYWARD PAST

For the Angry Sparrow

PROLOGUE

THE SINGLE GIRL'S TO-DO LIST
All roads lead to Rome and there is only one goal here.
He sits proudly at number 10!
1. Get a job
2. Get a flat
3. Get a wax
4. Get a tan
5. Get a hairdo
6. Get a cool new wardrobe
7. Get a gym membership
8. Get a great dance teacher
9. Get a gag for her polo-playing brothers
10. Get a (non-polo-playing) man

As THE only girl in a family of four polo-playing brothers I've had enough—and I mean ENOUGH!—of whips, spurs and raging machismo morning, noon and night.

CHAPTER ONE

Get a job

Not exactly the job I imagined, but I have my reasons. What are these reasons?

Actually, I landed the dream job: management trainee in a top London hotel. It was the icing on the cake after achieving a good degree in Hotel Management back home in Argentina, where a career in hospitality seemed the obvious choice to me after years honing my craft on four demanding brothers. But I would rather eat my own feet than keep that dream job by sleeping with a slime-ball concierge who tried to blackmail me by threatening to reveal who 'Anita Costa' really was.

People who knew me before this diary entry might ask, what has happened to wild child Lucia, the glamorous, glitzy, fun girl who was always the life and soul of the party, and who now seems to have sunk lower than a whore's drawers? If you're one of them you'd better read on.

You will note that the one thing I have retained is my sense of humour. Just as well, as right now things couldn't be much bleaker.

No one knew better than Lucia that a nightclub in daylight was a dismal, skanky place.

She should do. These past few days it had felt as if she spent most of her life on her hands and knees, scrubbing the sticky floor beneath a stark long-life bulb. Glittering and glamorous at night beneath the coloured lights, the club, located on the wild and rugged splendour of Cornwall's most popular coastline, was high on society's hot list—thanks to the many opportunities to see and be seen both in the club and on the fabulous beach, where the many sporting activities drew the best pecs around. Lucia's own dangerously charismatic polo-playing brothers had flaunted themselves in this same area when they were younger, with their hot friend Luke.

Luke...

Was this a good time to be thinking about more muscles and intelligence than was good for a man, captured in one devastatingly desirable package?

A man who was out of Lucia's reach?

And who just happened to be a polo player. Which meant contravening number ten on her to-do list before she had ticked off numbers two to nine.

'Don't you have enough to do?'

Lucia shot up as the club manager hove into view. Van Rickter had been a star on the club circuit in his youth, as he had been at pains to explain to Lucia when she had first begged him for a job—any job. Now he was a middle-aged charmer with a chip on his shoulder the size of a rock, who liked nothing better than to bully his staff. Lucia quickly returned to scrubbing as Grace, another of Van Rickter's serfs, entered the club.

'I hear there's a big do on tonight,' Grace announced, dropping her bag on a nearby table. 'Wish I didn't have these sniffles. A red nose and leaking eyes doesn't do much for tips. I was hoping to meet someone fabulous tonight who would take me away from all this—'

As Grace gestured around Lucia reflected that not so long

ago just the mention of a 'big do' would have been a call to arms. She had loved nothing better than to tease and flirt and dance. With four brothers ready to flatten any man who so much as looked at her the wrong way, she had grown up with no concept of danger when she turned it on, and had felt free to be as flirtatious as she liked. Her instant reaction to the merest suggestion of a party would have been on with the five-inch heels, the dress at least a size too small, followed swiftly by slap, glitter, lashes and nails, all topped off by the studiously perfected party pout. But that was then and this was now, and things were very different now.

Turning to Grace, Lucia thought her friend looked unusually pale tonight. 'Let me take your shift if you're not feeling well,' she suggested.

'Another shift straight after this one?' Grace shook her head in firm refusal 'You haven't stopped working since you got here. You'll make yourself ill if you go on like this. Put on your heels tonight, walk in like you own the place, see who's around. Save one for me if there are any likely men.'

Inwardly Lucia shuddered, but as Grace laughed she wiped her hot face on her sleeve and joined in the merriment. Grace had no idea what had happened to Lucia in London, and Lucia wasn't about to burden her new friend with details of that experience.

'Uh-oh, here comes trouble,' Grace warned as Van Rickter returned.

While Grace hurried into the back to get changed for work, Van Rickter picked on Lucia. 'Hey, Anita from the block,' he sneered. 'Put some elbow grease into that scrubbing. I can always find someone to replace you.' With an ugly laugh, he spun on his Cuban heels.

Everyone at the club knew her as Anita. It was the name of Lucia's favourite Puerto Rican character from the musical *West Side Story*. Finding a surname had been easy. Sitting in a coffee bar, she'd thought, *Just lose the 'a'*. So Lucia Acosta had become Anita Costa.

Why the subterfuge?

It wasn't possible to have people treat you normally, let alone strike out for independence, when your four polo-playing brothers featured on every billboard in town.

Resting her hands on the small of her aching back, Lucia dreamed of Argentina and the endless freedom of the pampas. Her warm, safe home in South America had never seemed further away, especially when it turned out that she had a real talent for jumping out of the frying pan into the fire. Her life, since that rogue concierge in London had made staying on at her job there impossible, had been one long slide down. It made no difference that she came from a wealthy family, and anyway, she was determined to go it alone.

'Okay?' Grace trilled as she hurried past with a crate of drinks.

'Never more so.'

Brushing her hair back, Lucia returned to scrubbing. After London she was glad to have a job at a club where no one knew her. Before she died, her mother had used to say to Lucia, 'Keep your wits about you.' Well, she'd certainly failed at that in London, believing the concierge was her friend.

It was hard to believe her mother had been killed almost ten years ago in a tragic flood. Demelza Acosta had been Cornish, which was why the family had always holidayed in St Oswalds. And why Lucia had fled here, she supposed, seeking refuge in the one corner of England where she re-membered being truly happy.

Lucia's head dipped over her scrubbing brush as Van Rickter came into view.

'It's your lucky day, Anita,' he observed sarcastically. 'I've sent Grace home. No one wants to be served cocktails by a waitress with a runny nose, so you're on bar duty tonight.

And don't even *think* of complaining that your cleaning shift doesn't end until seven,' he warned. 'You'll have plenty of time to get ready.'

Half an hour to race over to the caravan, hose herself down in cold water and get back to the club. If she didn't stop to eat it should be possible. 'That's fine with me.' She needed the money.

Van Rickter's piggy eyes almost disappeared into folds of unnaturally pale flesh as he eyed her suspiciously. 'Make sure you clean yourself up. And put some hand cream on. Those wrinkled mitts are enough to put anyone off their champagne.'

'I will,' she said, flashing a smile she knew would rattle Van Rickter far more than an exhausted look. She got tips on the bar.

Being nice and clean was more important for work than a full stomach. No one wanted a stinky server leaning over them, and she sure as hell wouldn't get any tips, Lucia reasoned, teeth chattering as she tied her wild black hair back neatly. She had just showered in shriekingly cold water in the beat-up caravan that came with her other job, and with ice on the insides of the windows it would take some considerable time before she warmed up.

Yes, she'd landed not one but two jobs—though the one that came with the caravan thrown in was rather more complicated than her work at the club, as she didn't get paid. Not yet. She was trying to help Margaret, the old lady who owned the Sundowner Guest House and Holiday Park, where Lucia had stayed as a child, to get back on her feet.

Teeth chattering, she rubbed herself down on a rough towel whilst shooting anxious glances at Grace's uniform. The tiny cocktail waitress ensemble looked far too small. She had put on a bit of weight since coming to Cornwall, having been plied with more Cornish cream teas than was good for her by Margaret. Not that she hadn't been what you might call voluptuous to start with.

Thanks to her handsome Argentinian father and her Cornish mother Lucia had been built to withstand not just the terrifying winds of the pampas but the frigid cold of a Cornish winter—genes that had made her infamous polo-playing brothers giants amongst men, but which had left *her* with the short straw. Now she was more a dumpy style of windbreak. Not that being curvy had seemed to put men off in the past. In fact at one time she'd used to have men—for men read her brothers' approved friends—eating out of her hand. Safe to say in London that hand had been well and truly bitten off.

Her brothers had definitely snaffled all the best growing genes, Lucia reflected as she heaved and tugged on Grace's minuscule boob-tube. Lucia was five foot three, while each of her brothers was at least a foot taller. Their width was breathtaking, whilst hers was merely distance across.

And that distance had never seemed greater, Lucia concluded, as she attempted to stuff one breast inside the elasticated boob-tube only to have the other spring out. And she had yet to tackle Grace's hot pants. Malevolently gleaming silver beneath the flickering light, they taunted her in silent reproach for a diet high on cheap and comforting junk food.

Having finally managed to subdue both breasts, she approached the hot pants warily, like an enemy that had to be put in its place.

Ouch!

The hot pants were definitely in place.

In tank top and jeans, ripped, tanned and pumped after exercise, Luke Forster was reclining with his cowboy boots crossed on an ornate coffee table at his hotel suite at the Grand Hotel in St Oswalds when he took a call from Argentina.

'Do me a favour and look Lucia up while you're there in Cornwall?' Luke's closest friend, Nacho Acosta asked him after they had finished discussing their latest polo match.

'Lucia's in Cornwall?'

'That's what she told me,' Nacho confirmed.

Luke stalled. *Must I?* Was his first thought. Lucia was Nacho's sister, and more trouble than any man needed. As Nacho recited Lucia's number he processed some swift mental imagery that seemed to centre mainly on Lucia's breasts.

That was *so* wrong. Nacho was his best friend and Lucia was the nearest thing Luke had to a sister. Breasts were definitely off the menu.

Lucia's breasts were pretty spectacular.

'She's gone off radar again, Luke.'

He shook himself round to take in what Nacho was saying.

'Though this time my sister *has* been good enough to leave a voicemail with the news that she's revisiting old haunts.'

Luke groaned inwardly. He was doing the same thing, so bang went his excuse not to look for her. Raking tense fingers through his thick brown hair, he added a couple of days to an already crammed schedule. Juggling wide-ranging business interests with his family's huge charitable foundation, as well as playing polo at the international level, demanded enough of his time without going on some wild goose chase looking for Nacho's wayward sister. It wasn't as if Lucia going off radar was anything new. The only female in a family with four forceful brothers, Lucia had broken away as soon as she could, quickly gaining the reputation of being a party girl extraordinaire.

'I know she's all grown up now, but I still feel responsible for her,' Nacho was explaining. 'You will do this for me, won't you, Luke?'

How could he refuse? Nacho had assumed responsibility for his siblings when their parents were killed in a flood, which had worked out great for Lucia's brothers, who were all older than Lucia, and had been okay for Lucia to begin with. But when she'd hit her teens…

'I'll find her,' he confirmed. 'If she's revisiting old haunts, what about school?'

'Which school?' Nacho demanded.

They both laughed.

Super-bright and super-bad, Lucia had run several headmistresses ragged. 'If she's in Cornwall,' he murmured, thinking out loud, 'it shouldn't be hard to find her. The village is dead, apart from the club. Let me follow a hunch,' he said, remembering Lucia dancing at the wedding. *That chick could* move.

'I can't ask for more than that,' Nacho agreed.

They started talking polo again, but Lucia had taken up residence in Luke's head. Both their mothers were Cornish, which was how the two families had met each year, holidaying together at the same quaint guest house on the rugged Cornish coast. The Sundowner had excellent stables and immediate access to the beach, which had given it the edge over the rest of the local accommodation where Luke's parents were concerned. The Sundowner Guest House was intimate and private, plus the owner's quirky take on hospitality, treating every family as her own, meant it offered something money couldn't buy.

Luke loved Cornwall. He was glad to be back here doing business. It was the one place he felt free. Maybe he hadn't realised it as a boy, but when he'd galloped across the beach with Lucia's brothers he'd been true to himself. Now he was successful in his own right he wanted to recapture those feelings of elation and freedom.

'Let me know as soon as you hear something, Luke,' Nacho pressed him, adding, 'I envy you being back in St Oswalds. Do you remember tearing up the beach on those wild ponies?'

'How could I forget?' He liked that Nacho felt the same. 'Would you come back if I reinstated polo on the beach?'

'You bet I would,' Nacho assured him.

With one of the top polo players in the world on board, his plan was already starting to take shape, but as Nacho applied more pressure for him to bring polo back to Cornwall Luke was still thinking about Lucia.

He and Lucia were so different. Luke was an only child, brought up preppy and obedient, and when he was a boy the Acostas had seemed an exotic bunch to him, with their dark flashing eyes and outstanding horsemanship. He had made a point of riding on the beach at the same time as the brothers, wanting them to see his own skill on a horse. Nacho had taught him how to stand on a horse's back while it galloped, nearly killing him in the process, while Lucia had merely tossed her glorious black hair in his face and turned a dismissive back.

Remember those eyes when Lucia flashed a challenge? Those dark, mischievous eyes...

Damn those eyes! Lucia was more trouble than she was worth. 'I'll be in touch when I've got something to tell you, Nacho.'

'That's good enough for me, Luke.'

He exchanged the usual pleasantries and ended the call with Lucia firmly fixed in his mind.

He was still thinking about her later that day, remembering the last time he'd seen her at an Acosta family wedding. Expecting a temperamental teen, he had found a woman who was all grown up. And *hot*. The way she had sashayed up to him, only to veer away at the very last moment on the pretext of seeking out one of her brothers, had left him with an ache in his groin and sweet revenge on his mind.

Forget Lucia, Luke told himself sternly as he waged the endless razor war on stubble that refused to surrender. Tonight he was meeting an attractive blonde who ran an events company, which dovetailed nicely with his plan to start investigating the possibility of reinstating the annual Polo on the Beach event, which had been started way back by Lucia's father. His conversation with Nacho had crystallised his plans, and though it was a setback to find St Oswalds so run down, construction was one of the main planks of his business, so it made perfect sense for him to regenerate the village and bring the world back to its door.

And Lucia? What part would she play?

So much for forgetting about Lucia, Luke concluded, studying his freshly shaved face in the mirror. Shaving was a necessary habit rather than a purposeful exercise. Stubble was already shading his face, making him look more piratical than ever. His East Coast American father liked to protest that he could never understand where Luke's looks came from. 'All that thick, dark hair and the swarthy complexion…and those muscles! So vulgar.' That was his father's verdict. At which point he would cast an accusing glance at Luke's mother and tell her that it must be her side of the family to blame.

That was the link between him and Lucia. They were both outsiders. Lucia was the girl yearning for independence in a household dominated by four alpha males, while he was the musclebound son of Princeton. Quite how that would help him combine a business dinner with a blonde with a hunt for a wild child on the loose remained to be seen.

Lucia's body had just gone into meltdown. *Luke Forster was in the club.* It wasn't possible…

Unless there were two formidable warrior-type men who stood head and shoulders above every other man in the place, with the looks to make any pretty-boy film star pack up his bags and go home, it was a rock-hard certainty. No two men on earth looked as good as that.

So what was Luke Forster doing here?

Rooted to the spot, with a tray of drinks balanced precariously in her shaking hands, Lucia was hiding in the shadows by the bar, oblivious to the barman yelling, 'Get a move on, Anita. There's another order waiting. You know we're short-handed tonight, babe.'

'Move it, Anita!'

She leapt into action at the sound of Van Rickter's voice. Why couldn't the manager keep his voice down? Her name-change wouldn't fool Luke for a second. To make matters worse, Luke had a woman on his arm—a very glamorous woman. Lucia could just imagine them both laughing when Luke explained in his husky, mocking tone that Lucia was running away again, and this time with a name that reflected her interest in music and coffee.

'Thanks, darling,' the barman said as he passed another loaded tray across the bar. 'You're the best.'

She zipped away, taking the long route round to her table of customers to avoid Luke. She didn't want him to see her like this… Not just working here at the club. She would defend her right to work to the bitter end. But Luke knew her too well. He would sense how she'd changed. *Dirty… Defiled… Ashamed and afraid…*

But she was fighting back in her own time, and on her own terms.

Stamping down on the recent past, Lucia returned her thoughts to Luke. She had tried everything to eject Luke from her head, but nothing worked. The more she tried the more she wanted him, and everything had changed since the last time they had met when she had flirted so outrageously with him. She had invited trouble by living up to her wild-child image and now she had to pay the price. The woman on his arm was more Luke's type. Smart, sharp, businesslike and neatly packaged. Lucia doubted Luke's girlfriend would get herself into any awkward position outside a yoga class. Her only consolation was that the girl's improbably whitened teeth attracted the club's ultraviolet light in a way no one would want unless they suffered chronic delusions of being a torch.

'Where do you think you're going?'

Lucia froze at the sound of Van Rickter's voice. She had dumped the tray of empty glasses and had been hoping to make it to the stockroom before Luke spotted her. Rubbing her arms energetically, she said, 'Don't you think it's cold in here? I thought I'd turn the heating up.'

'Put some more clothes on while you're at it,' Van sneered. 'The new uniform was designed with slimmer girls than you in mind. There should be some of the old shapeless ones in the back.'

'That's where I'm heading,' she said brightly. Sloughing off Van's insults, she glanced anxiously over her shoulder. Thankfully Luke was still in deep conversation with the blonde. Luke wasn't just her brothers' closest friend, he was a fully paid-up member of their over-protective, pain-in-the-ass, let's-keep-Lucia-at-ten-years-old-for-ever gang. He certainly wasn't someone she wanted to see her dressed in too-tight silver hot pants and an X-rated top.

'Wait!' Van Rickter barked in a way she was certain must draw Luke's attention. 'If you're off the floor longer than five minutes, you're fired. Do I make myself clear?'

'Crystal,' Lucia said, backing towards the stockroom.

'Find the biggest uniform you can' was Van's parting shot.

'Thank you. I will.'

She disappeared behind the door with a gust of relief. She couldn't care less what Van Rickter thought about her. Ever since London she had wanted to be thought a sexless amoeba without cheekbones, breasts or a waist. Seeing Luke had only reinforced that desperate wish. Far from wanting to flirt with him, she would happily turn her back on all men with the greatest relief. And whatever sort of mess her life was in, *she* would sort it out. Not her brothers. And definitely not Luke.

Last year's uniform wasn't much better on her than this year's, but at least it had a skirt. Well, almost. Wriggling into it, she plucked the matching satin shirt from its hanger and slipped it on, tying it beneath her ample breasts. She hesitated over the grubby plastic camellia blossom she was supposed to pin behind her ear. There were limits.

She walked out of the stockroom straight into Luke. Just her luck—he was at the bar buying drinks. Now she couldn't breathe, let alone pull something out of the bag to defuse the shocked look in his eyes. 'Luke!' she said, feigning surprise as her heart threatened to explode. 'What are you doing here?'

'I might ask you the same question.' he said, taking a step back to eye her up and down.

Telling herself she was used to alpha males, having grown up with four of them, she lifted her chin. 'This is where we always go,' she said, gesturing around as if she was at the club with a huge gang of friends. This only succeeded in causing Luke's eyes to narrow with disbelief.

With shock crackling between them as Luke scoffed disbelievingly, she drank him in. Luke was the essence of male. Bigger and more powerful than the other men in the club, he was infinitely better looking. Luke had always been able to melt her with a glance—though at the moment that glance was doing its best to incinerate her, which for once rested more comfortably with Lucia than the smouldering, sexy look Luke was so good at. He was even bigger than she remembered—harder, tougher—though, as always, immaculately groomed, with shoulders wide enough to hoist an ox and hard-muscled legs that went on and on to…to a point from which she quickly averted her eyes.

While *she* had not only let herself go, but was wearing last year's shabby club uniform, with her hair scraped back and her face glowing red and shiny beneath the lights. Perfect.

'Lucia?' Luke rapped sternly, staring down at her with knife-sharp eyes. 'Are you working here?'

Of course she should have said, *What's it to you?* But a row might draw attention and she couldn't afford to lose this job. 'No, of course I'm not working here,' she protested with a laugh, glancing around to make sure no one had heard Luke calling her by her real name. 'I come here so often they let me hang my coat in the stockroom.'

'Really?' Luke drawled, with an even more contemptuous expression in his brooding amber gaze.

'Okay, from time to time,' she admitted, brushing it off as she continued to stare at a face that was mesmerising in its harsh masculine beauty. If you wanted *hard* there was no better hard to be had than Luke Forster—as her yearning and thoroughly confused body would now attest. But Van was prowling, Lucia noticed. 'Gin and orange for your friend?' she suggested as the blonde, having exited the restroom, made a beeline for them.

'I have ordered our drinks, thank you,' Luke said coolly. 'Vanessa,' he murmured, in what Lucia considered an unnecessarily indulgent tone, 'I'd like you to meet an old friend of mine.'

'Not so much of the old,' Lucia joked weakly, feeling awkward and ridiculously exposed when she compared herself to Luke's neatly styled friend. The blonde was even prettier close up, and was hanging on to Luke's arm as if her life depended on it.

'Do you work here?' Vanessa enquired, visibly relaxing once she had assessed Lucia and found her lacking in—well, practically everything.

'I help out here occasionally,' Lucia said carefully.

'How nice to have such a...sociable job.' The blonde looked

at Luke for approval of her assessment, but Luke was too busy studying Lucia.

Van, having spotted money, was sniffing around. 'Have you seen our new casino yet?' he crowed.

Van clearly imagined he had found a high-roller in Luke, but Lucia knew Luke had never gambled in his life, and rarely drank. Having summoned another of his serfs—a far more attractive cocktail waitress than Lucia—Van ushered the small group away.

The only good thing about it, Lucia mused from the shelter of the bar, was that Van was so drunk on the scent of money he had chosen to walk backward in front of Luke—until he collided with a table and then had to turn and chase after his big-striding guest.

The crowd on the dance floor fell back at Luke's advance like the Red Sea parting, and Luke paused at the entrance to the casino just long enough to shoot a stare at Lucia that assured her this wasn't nearly over yet.

CHAPTER TWO

Get a flat

Admittedly, this is not quite the accommodation I had in mind. But, again, there are reasons. And holiday parks are all the rage, offering an unparalleled level of life-style, according to the ads I've read in magazines. Sadly, my des res is a leaking tin can on wheels, with no discernible braking system, parked in a ramshackle field on the edge of a crumbling cliff a good half-mile walk from the shelter of the guest house. Try that out for size in a sleet storm in winter.

SHE spent the rest of the shift swinging like a pendulum between kicking herself because Luke had caught her out and wondering how on earth to explain to her brothers' clearly bemused friend what she was doing there—without actually telling him what had happened, that was. Why hadn't she been frank with him and looked to Luke to keep her safe? He was the next best thing to a brother, wasn't he? Why hadn't she told him the truth?

Because it was none of Luke's damn business!

And because she had never felt more ashamed or more soiled in her life. He would never look at her the same way again if he knew... She couldn't be further from her dream of building her own life, independent of Luke and her brothers,

Lucia realised as Van switched off the soft lights in the club after another long night, turning on the harsh glare of factory-style strip-lighting.

There was a song about a girl from South America who was tall and young and lovely. Lucia had used to hum it beneath her breath when she was a pre-teen, never dreaming she would turn into the *other* girl from Ipanema—the one who was short and a bit too fat, plain and olive-skinned. And stupid. She had to be stupid to have got herself into such a mess in London. How could she go home and tell them the truth now? It was all too humiliating, too shameful.

So she would ride this storm out like any other, Lucia told herself firmly. She just hadn't fathomed out how yet.

She had been monumentally thrown at seeing Luke again, Lucia reasoned as she helped the barman clean the bar. She *was* making the climb back, though, however long it was taking, and she should cut herself some slack. Tonight the best thing she could do was to concentrate on cleaning up and earning a night's pay.

His attention on the blonde hadn't so much slipped as fallen down a ravine—a ravine with Lucia at the bottom of it. To say he was shocked at seeing her working here would be putting it mildly. It was a world away from the last time he'd seen her, dancing so hotly he hadn't been able to take his eyes off her. How had she gone from that to working for a toad like Van Rickter? How was that supposed to further Lucia's career? And where was she living? Who was she spending time with? What had happened to the girl who had blown him out of the water with her sass, her dancing, her brilliant smile, her world-class flirting, her breasts? Okay, so the breasts were still pretty amazing, but the rest...

What the hell had happened to Lucia?

The thought that Van Rickter might have something to do

with it made the hackles rise on the back of his neck. His call to Nacho could wait. There were a few enquiries he wanted to make first.

He glanced round impatiently as Vanessa waved an empty glass in his face. 'The club's closed,' he pointed out sharply, knowing he was the one to blame for hanging on to watch Lucia.

Making his excuses before the evening became even more uncomfortable than it had already been, he called a cab for the blonde and took Van Rickter into the back room to make a few things clear to him.

'How long has that girl called Lucia worked here?'

'Lucia?' Van Rickter seemed genuinely confused. 'There's no one called Lucia working here,' he protested, with a shifty, guilty look.

'The dark-haired girl with the attitude and —'

'Oh, you mean Anita,' Van Rickter said on a wave of relief. 'At least that's what she calls herself here,' he said, quickly covering himself in case Lucia had done something wrong. 'Don't tell me she's an illegal?' Van exclaimed, wiping his brow as if hiring vulnerable people for cash and far less than the minimum wage had never occurred to him.

'I mean Anita,' Luke agreed offhandedly. 'I must have misheard her name,' He might be all out of patience with Lucia, but this was private business. He wasn't going to give Van Rickter anything that he could hurt Lucia with, or make money out of.

'I could arrange a meeting, if you like,' Van Rickter said, in a way that made Luke's pupils shrink to arrowheads. 'All the girls owe me…'

I bet they do, Luke thought with distaste.

'She has a second job at the local guest house,' Van Rickter revealed, toadying up to him. 'The Sundowner? You might have heard of it. Maybe the owner there can tell you more.'

Luke hid his rush of triumph. Lucia wouldn't be using the alias Anita at the guest house, where the owner knew her, so Margaret must be in on Lucia's life plan—whatever that might be. But there was something else worrying him. If he hadn't known better he would have said Lucia had flinched from him, almost as if she had some communicable disease. That wasn't the girl he knew—the girl who would happily take any man down with her repartee. So what the hell was going on?

In spite of his distaste at being forced to discuss Lucia with a man like Van Rickter, he was amused at the thought of Lucia choosing the name of a Puerto Rican firecracker in a musical. It made him think back to her brothers, yelling at her to turn the caterwauling down when they had wanted heavy metal to rule the house. He could imagine Lucia had dreamed of being Anita, a woman free to express herself without four brothers drowning her out—though in his opinion Lucia had far more going for her than a fantasy figure.

Kill those thoughts. Lucia was trouble. Whatever mess she had got herself into this time, it wasn't up to him to sort it out. He'd tell Nacho he'd found her and then his job was done.

Lucia had a second job? Luke mused, turning to stare at the entrance to the club. No wonder she looked exhausted. Two lousy jobs in the wilds of Cornwall didn't come close to equalling one good job in the heart of London. So what had happened to the management position at the top London hotel Nacho had been telling him about? He consoled himself with the thought that whatever she was hiding he would find out. Lucia was living at the Sundowner, and Margaret, the owner, was a big part of his plan to revive the area.

'Luke…'

She was thrashing about in bed in that half-world between sleeping and waking where anything was possible—even a man making love to her. But this wasn't any man.

Shifting restlessly on what passed for her pillow, she pulled the scratchy blanket round her shoulders and slipped deeper into the world of dreams, where her body was still capable of quivering with awareness, with warmth and with arousal—where Luke's brooding amber gaze needed no explanation and the care in his big, strong hands was all the reassurance she needed.

Seeing Luke again tonight had been bound to lead to this, Lucia's drifting mind soothed. Her eyes were open and yet they were closed. She was sleeping, surely? The air was misty with a golden glow. Candles were flickering. Seductive scents tickled her nostrils. Luke was stripped to the waist and leaning over her. He was as magnificent as ever. His golden torso, so powerful and so shielding, made her feel small, made her feel safe, made her feel that anything was possible—even Luke looking at her with desire in his eyes...

Thrashing her head on the pillow, she knew this was wrong. Luke was taboo. She should not be lying here naked with him. Luke was older, established, confident, experienced. Luke was her brothers' friend—upright and principled.

Her body didn't care about any of that and responded urgently. Reaching out, she mapped the wealth of muscle from his shoulders to his iron-hard belly, glorying in his strength. And when Luke quivered beneath her touch she revelled in her power over him. But Luke refused to accept her dominance and, swinging her beneath him, brushed his fingertips across her breasts, watching without pity as she gasped for air and arced towards him, seeking more contact.

What was she doing? Luke was built on a heroic scale, and when he discovered the truth about her he would throw her off in disgust.

Luke knew how much she wanted him. Holding her gaze, he caressed her, and she groaned as pleasure spiralled through her body. Reaching up, she laid her palm against his stubble-roughened cheek. Luke answered by teasing her lips apart and taking her mouth in a scorching reminder of what else he'd like to do to her.

'I have no other duty but to please you,' he said.

Quite right too, she thought, though the longing to pleasure Luke was overcoming her, and to be pleasured by him, to forget her fear. But just as she reached for him he slowed the pace. Turning away, he poured champagne, then reached for some fruit in the bowl by the bed. He dipped a ripe berry in melted chocolate before holding it to her lips. She sat forward. He took it away. He moved to kiss her. She moved away. Luke's eyes held so much understanding, and when his lips claimed hers he tasted of strawberries and chocolate. Gaining in confidence, she rubbed her naked breasts against his chest and felt her nipples tighten. Drawing deeply on his warm male scent, she placed her hands flat against Luke's hard, hot torso and drew him down.

'Tell me what you want, Lucia.'

'Kiss me,' she begged, reaching up.

'Is that all?'

'It's enough.'

'I don't believe you.'

As Luke cupped her with his hand, almost but not quite granting her the contact she craved, a wave of pleasure stole away her fear. But then he drove his thigh between her legs and demanded harshly, 'What's wrong, Anita?'

Anita?

She shrieked in terror as the fantasy collapsed and instead of Luke the fat, flabby, pale-skinned concierge loomed naked and aroused above her, red-faced and lecherous. His reptilian eyes glistened yellow in the light, while his fat red lips, wet with saliva, just as she remembered them, were drawn back in a snarl over rotting teeth. She fought him, fighting furiously for her honour, for her life—

Waking with a start, Lucia sucked in a sharp breath, staring round fearfully. It took her a moment to realise where she was. The caravan slowly took on a reassuring form. There was no concierge. There was no Luke. There was no satin bed-linen. There were just bobbly grey sheets, and she had been slithering about on top of one of her magazines. Luke hadn't been feeding her chocolate sauce and fruit. And there certainly wasn't any champagne. There were just some dregs of hot chocolate left in the flask on a shelf by the bed.

She was still shaking as the nightmare faded. Climbing out of bed, she realised the dream was the closest she'd come to sex with Luke—was ever likely to come to sex with Luke—and even in her dreams she couldn't get it right.

Because the concierge had taken over.

Perhaps it would always be like that from now on. Perhaps her dream of becoming a strong, independent woman was just a pipe dream. Perhaps she would never be able to make love properly, because the concierge would always be waiting in the wings to spoil things for her.

And after a dream like that, how could she ever face Luke again?

It was eleven o' clock on a Friday night and the club was heaving. A whole seven Luke-free days had passed. And that was good.

Was it?

Yes, of course it was. She could do without any more of those dreams seeing Luke seemed to provoke. He had probably returned to the States by now, after taking the same trip down memory lane in Cornwall that she had. She could only hope for Luke's sake he had had a better result. She was currently putting in a second shift as another cocktail waitress had gone off sick, and she was so tired she was seriously considering nabbing a couple of cocktail sticks from the bar to prop her eyes open. There must be a convention on at the Grand, Lucia guessed, as more people poured in through the door.

'Anita.'

Van was approaching. There had been a distinct improvement in Van's mood since Luke's visit. He couldn't take the risk that Lucia had friends in high places, she supposed, though that had been wearing a bit thin this evening, as if Van suspected her influential friend might have deserted her finally.

The holiday had definitely ended, Lucia concluded, as Van snapped, 'There's been a spillage on the dance floor. Do something about it, will you?' Van's piggy eyes continued darting back and forth as he spoke, counting money as it walked through the door. *'Now,'* he spelled out, turning to glare at her. 'We have some important patrons stopping by tonight.'

'Yes, sir,' Lucia murmured, hurrying away to get her mop and bucket.

'And, Anita?'

'Yes?' She stopped and turned around.

'You need to lose weight.'

She nodded agreement. Van was always right. That was the mindset you had to have if you wanted a quiet life at the club. But in this instance Van *was* right. She felt humiliated in the too-tight boob tube and hot pants ensemble, over which she overflowed with all the glorious abundance of a chocolate fountain. But since Van had made her revert back to the original cocktail waitress uniform so she 'blended in', as he put it, she would just have to suck it up.

Emerging from the stockroom with her cleaning tackle, she grabbed a clean apron from a hook by the door. She would have preferred a tent, but that might have looked a bit obvious, and at least the apron partially concealed her body.

She had to put out cones to keep the area clear so no one would slip on the dance floor while she was working. She'd done plenty of clean-ups at the club, but this one was particularly revolting. Suffice it to say unmentionable substances, still with the distinct tang of brandy and cola about them, had spread widely across the black glass tiles. She was making good progress while customers gyrated around her unconcerned. She was invisible. Wasn't that great?

Not so great when she got stomped on a couple of times. But she was nearly finished.

Lucia's heart bounced once and then stopped. There was only one man who would have the balls to wear cowboy boots with a sharp Italian suit. She stiffened as a pair of very large feet halted within inches of her nose.

Important patron? Van had got that right. Conscious that her XXL silver-clad backside was poking up in the air, she quickly drew it down and remained quite still, as if she might somehow become invisible again.

But sadly no.

'Lucia?'

How could her life get any worse?

Luke Forster, Lucia's childhood crush, and more recently her erotic dream buddy, was back.

CHAPTER THREE

Where in my list does it say that one of the bad boys of polo can crack his whip over my head while I'm on my hands and knees in front of him?

Blech! That does not sound good.

Did that possibility even cross my mind when I was a fourteen-year-old dreamer with only gallant knights in shining armour ahead of me?

No. It did not.

'UP.'

People turned to stare. Luke's voice sounded like a pistol crack, blotting out the music as well as the overheated chatter in the club.

'Hello, Luke,' Lucia said mildly, determined there wouldn't be a scene. Van would sack her on the spot. And wouldn't Luke relish ammunition like that when he made his report to her brothers? 'How nice to see you again.' With clothes on, she amended silently, trying hard not to blink.

'Imagine my surprise to see you here *working*,' Luke countered with bite. He returned her upturned gaze with an expressionless stare.

Attack was the only form of defence in this situation. Why was she still down on her knees? Standing, she said coolly, 'You didn't think to say goodbye last time you were in the club. Oh, no—I forgot,' she added. 'You had better things to do.' A spear of inconvenient jealousy hit her as she looked in vain for the blonde.

'She's not here,' Luke said, reading her with ease. 'And you're leaving.'

'I beg your pardon?' Now she was upset. One of the upsides of seeing Luke again was that it had restored some of her old fire. She hadn't broken free of her brothers only to be ordered about by Luke!

'You heard me,' Luke said stonily.

Breaking eye contact, she reached for her bucket.

'You're leaving that where it is,' he rapped.

'No!' Luke's big tanned hand seized hold of her arm, and it was bad enough seeing those sensitive fingers sinking into pale, plump flesh without remembering the magic those hands had wrought in her dream...

This was reality, Lucia reminded herself sharply.

But wasn't this what she had waited for all her life? Luke riding to her rescue. Luke holding her. Luke...

'Get off me,' she fired out furiously, shaking herself free. 'I'm not a horse you can grab hold of and lead where you like. I make my own plans, Luke. And I'm working. Do you want me to lose my job?'

Luke's arrogant head dipped so he could glare straight into her eyes. 'I would love you to lose your job,' he assured her grimly.

'I come off shift at three a.m. I can talk to you then, but not before,' she said, aware that Van the Terrible was lurking in the shadows, watching them.

Picking up her mop and bucket, she stalked off the dance floor before Luke had the chance to say a word.

There was only one small consolation in all of this. Her body might be trembling like a leaf, but she was earning a living, and however small that living might be when compared to

Luke's vast income she was living independently. *Two* small consolations, Lucia conceded with surprise. Confronting Luke hadn't frightened her. She hadn't backed down and slithered away to do his bidding. She had felt as if she'd been in a perpetual state of fear since London—finally she was beginning to feel alive again.

So she didn't need him. *Good.* He shouldn't get involved. He would call Nacho—let him take over. Lucia was wild and had set herself on a very different path from him. He was all about polo and business, and had no intention of being distracted or pulled down by anyone. Lucia was clearly on a downward trajectory. With every advantage in the world, she had chosen to work in a club.

Really? Did he believe that?

All he knew for certain at this point was that in his family no one went against expectation, and feelings were curbed as stringently as any horse in a dressage arena. Lucia was composed entirely of emotion. She was an untameable Acosta. He should put her out of his mind for good

Which was easier said than done. He was becoming increasingly worried about her, and in spite of the cold facts he owed Nacho.

Was that all?

So she was attractive. He would soon tire of all the drama.

Wasn't it entertaining to be around someone with so much character for a change?

Didn't he love to hunt?

He liked the chase best of all.

What the hell was he thinking?

Lucia was the kid sister of his closest friend. She was out of bounds. And, in the unlikely event that he found himself in the mood for a walk on the wild side, he'd choose someone as worldly as he was—not some pampered Argentinian princess.

Who wasn't too proud to get down on her hands and knees and scrub a filthy club if that was what it took.

And who was one hell of a good-looking woman, Luke conceded, even in the extraordinary outfit Lucia was forced to wear at work.

All the more reason for him to keep his distance. With his blood boiling in his veins she was safer away from him.

Three o'clock in the morning came and went. The last patron had left the club. They had swept up and tidied and Luke had gone. She'd been too busy to notice when he left. He had left with the blonde, she presumed, feeling sick inside. He definitely hadn't remembered what day it was today.

So what? Why should she care if Luke had forgotten it was her birthday? She didn't need him. Luke Forster could go to hell in a bucket for all she cared.

'Didn't your birthday start at midnight?' Grace asked, giving Lucia's arm a squeeze as they left the club together.

'How did you know?' Lucia asked as they took shelter for a moment before braving the rain.

'I know everything about you,' Grace teased fondly.

Including Lucia's real name. Grace was too good a friend for Lucia to want to deceive her. 'So you've heard the party-girl rumours too?'

Grace laughed. 'You don't know the meaning of the word. You're not a party girl any more than I am, Lucia. But some of our friends at the club seem to think we should lighten up a bit.'

'I hope you're not referring to Van Rickter?'

Grace frowned. 'I wouldn't call him a friend, exactly, but there *are* other nice people working at the club.'

'What are you hiding under your jacket?' Lucia enquired as they crossed the road.

'We had a whip-round for your birthday,' Grace explained, starting to smile.

'What is it?' Lucia asked, her curiosity well and truly roused.

'I'm not saying. I don't want to spoil the surprise. But I will tell you this much—everyone seems determined to tempt at least one of us off the straight and narrow this year.'

'It might take a bit longer than that for me,' Lucia admitted, shivering as the cold wind whipped around her.

'Don't be such a defeatist,' Grace teased. 'A lot can happen quickly if you're lucky.'

Lucia huffed as Grace squeezed her arm again, and then both girls screamed as they sploshed through an icy puddle in the middle of the road.

'I stuck a couple of mags in the bag as well,' Grace called out as they parted company at the entrance to the Sundowner Holiday Park. 'You might recognise one of the centrefolds. You were talking to him in the club.'

Lucia's heart went crazy with excitement. The centrefold was hardly going to be Van Rickter—unless the magazine in question was *Amphibian World*.

She ran all the way to the caravan and, throwing her shoulder against the buckled door, launched herself inside. Dropping her things on the floor, she snatched the magazines out of the gift bag and flung herself onto the lumpy bunk. Leafing through as fast as she could, she stalled at the centre page of the second magazine.

Luke Forster was *ROCK!*'s Torso of the Year.

Dropping the magazine, she threw herself back against the cold tin wall. 'You blue-blooded hypocrite!' Her main gripe was not how Luke looked—which was pretty spectacular by any standards—but the way he behaved when he was around her, as if he were a paragon of all the virtues. 'So you're incorruptible, are you?'

Now, this was worrying. Not only was she talking to herself, but she was involving a magazine in the conversation. With an angry huff, she plucked the gum from her mouth and stuck Luke's centrefold to the wall. 'Take that!' A thump from her fist secured it. Standing back, she had to concede Luke's centrefold *did* brighten things up a bit.

So where was he? Lucia wondered, going through her nightly routine of getting ready for bed in the freezing caravan by piling on more clothes. If Luke was still in Cornwall he was probably tucked up in a nice warm room at the Grand by now—with the blonde. *Ack!* And if he thought about Lucia at all it would only be to wonder if she was ready to go home yet.

'No, I'm not ready,' she snarled, glaring at Luke's poster. 'And I'm not giving up. I can't give up. I can't go home. Not like this.…'

Their nice, warm kitchen in Argentina, where the roof never leaked and the floor was never cold, and she had never once had to pick ice off the insides of the windows...

Unscrewing the top of the flask of hot chocolate that Margaret left on the table each night, she scowled at Luke's centrefold as she gulped the warm liquid down. She tried not to think about the list of goals she had intended to achieve by now—goals Lucia had been so confident were achievable when she was fourteen.

Reaching beneath the bed, she drew out the precious tote full of memories and extracted the battered notebook in which, as a dreamy-eyed teen, she had written down her innermost hopes and dreams. She didn't often do this. She saved it for when things were really bad. The bag of dreams, as she called the old canvas tote, was her comforter. It contained her journal from when she was fourteen, and her rather more neglected journal from now. She pulled the old one out and started to read.

It is imperative *to follow this list to the letter if I'm* ever *going to break free from Conan the Barbarian and his gang of galloping gauchos—otherwise known as my brothers...*

Lucia smiled as she read the messy list, with all its scribbles and crossings-out. It was hard to believe she had ever been so naïve. Most of her ideas had been based on articles she'd read in teen magazines, which of course were essential reading for fourteen-year-olds with everything to learn. She would have to completely re-jig the list. Get a wax *after* she'd got a man? Well, that was wrong to start with. And, the way she felt right now, getting a wax could be number two-hundred and thirty-six on next year's list. Yes, Luke was gorgeous, but...

No. She couldn't.

She just couldn't, that's all.

But just out of curiosity, and because trips down memory lane seemed to be in vogue right now, she straightened out the much-thumbed pages and began to read.

1. Get a job!—preferably promoting a bar, which is a great way to meet new people, according to *ROCK!* magazine
2. Get a flat!—something gorgeous and stylish in the best part of town. N.B. V. close to the bar!
3. Get a wax!

She remembered that last entry being based more on dreading what her rapidly changing body might do next rather than any horrific hirsute happenings. And how many times had that entry been deferred? And why did she still shift position nervously when she read it?

She pulled a face as she got up to check her top lip in

the mirror. Flopping back down again, she remembered her mother's pale face when a visit to the beautician loomed. Perhaps that was the answer to her waxing phobia. She could still hear her young self asking, 'Are you all right, Mama?' And her mother's response: 'You'll understand one day what it means to be a woman, Lucia, and what we have to go through for our men...' Hefty sigh at that point.

All sorts of images had flashed into Lucia's young brain—nostril-hair-plucking, blackhead-excising, even earwax-removal with one of those long, pointy things—but never had she imagined that her mother was referring to that most delicate of regions, let alone that some stranger was going to view her private bits close up prior to coating them in molten wax like some medieval torturer. And it didn't finish there—as Lucia had discovered in that invaluable teenage self-help tome known to one and all as *ROCK! Magazine*. Then this female Torquemada was going to rip away at those nether regions without so much as a by-your-leave.

Youch!

No way, José!

Back to the list. The next entry after wax, was

4. Get a tan

Lucia remembered a columnist in *ROCK!* insisting that this must be subtle—a mere sun-kissed whisper that would fool any man into thinking it was natural.

5. Get a cool new wardrobe!

One that did not include a bobbly polyester uniform in a shade that might once have been white, presumably.

6. Get a hairdo

This prompted another visit to the mirror, where she lifted up her haystack hair. Most people complained that their hair was too thin or too straight. She was currently experiencing the opposite problem, known as The Inexplicable Explosion of Frizz. Without her styling products and gadgets, and without money to get it done in a salon, she was on her own.

7. Get a gym membership

First off, gym memberships cost money. And there was a more important consideration: without the hairdo, the tan, the wax and the cool new wardrobe, she was never going to make it through the door of a decent gym.

8. Get a good dance teacher—for the Samba, preferably. Someone like the old gaucho Ignacio, on Nero Caracas's ranch. Judging by the way Ignacio vaulted the fence when I decided to ride Nero's fire-breathing monster stallion bareback, Ignacio has still got some moves in him!
9. Get a gag for her polo-playing brothers—so they can't share any embarrassing secrets with any men I might attract once I've completed all of the above.
10. Get a (non-polo-playing) man

And there the list ended. Lucia smiled as she remembered Ignacio teaching her to dance the Samba, and quite a few other dances as well, bringing his ancient ghetto blaster, as Ignacio had called his battered radio, to the hay barn, where she'd been able to blunder about undisturbed. Okay. Looking on the bright side. She was still podgy and in need of a sun-tan with a frizz ball on her head, but this babe could dance.

'Cheers, Margaret,' Lucia murmured, wrapping her frozen hands around the warm flask of chocolate. This small, kind act of someone who had so little made Lucia more determined than ever to help her elderly friend.

'And hello, Luke,' she added, addressing Luke's smouldering poster just inches from her bed.

Hopping out again, she took a closer look. *Wow* hardly covered it. Lucia's brothers frequently featured on billboards, but always in full polo rig and usually mounted on a horse. They were certainly never caught half-naked, sluicing themselves down, in a shot Lucia couldn't imagine strait-laced Luke agreeing to in a million years.

'You're full of surprises, aren't you?' she murmured, taking full inventory of Luke's previously hidden assets.

And then there was the pose. Brandishing a whip as he glared into the camera, Luke was naked to his washboard waist, his hard tanned torso accessorised by nothing more than sharp black stubble and a steel watch that could probably tell his position in relation to the moon. A pair of obscenely revealing riding breeches and knee-high leather boots completed an image guaranteed to make any girl's day.

Posters were a safe way to appreciate the finer points of one of the world's fittest men. She liked that. As she jumped about and blew on her hands to keep warm before hypothermia set in, Lucia guessed the only way Luke would have been caught out in a shot like that was through the involvement of her school friend and ruthless sister-in-law Holly. Holly was a journalist at *ROCK!* magazine, and had tamed—sorry—was *married* to Lucia's brother Ruiz. Capturing Luke in such a provocative pose would have been an incredible scoop for her.

Three cheers for Holly the reporter! Lucia concluded, chalking one up for the girls. She took another look at Luke's centrefold.

Goodness, Luke was big...

No wonder she was having erotic dreams. Trying hard not to fixate on Luke's clinging breeches and the improbable-sized bulge within, Lucia shook her head. She could admire all she liked, but it certainly would never happen now. It couldn't. *She* couldn't. One thing was sure: after this unveiling he could stick his disapproval the next time they met.

The next time they met?

There was nothing on her to-do list that ruled against meetings with an approved family friend, she reasoned, climbing into bed.

CHAPTER FOUR

*I wandered lonely as a cloud that floats o'er vales and
hill...*
   *I'm the only twenty-four-year-old I know who doesn't
need to take her pill.*
   Anon.
   ~~Are all poets destined to end up on the (remainder)
shelf?~~
   Pull yourself together, Lucia!

RESTING her cheek against the cold wet glass the next morning,
Lucia stopped scribbling in her journal and stared out of the
caravan window at the windswept shore. If she had wanted
distance from her brothers she had certainly got it here. She
missed them, but no way was she going to ask them for the
money to help Margaret. If she did she'd be right back to
square one. Yes, she loved her brothers, but Nacho especially
made no distinction between caring and smothering, which
had left her gasping for freedom in the shadow of four powerful men and their saintly friend Luke.

Luke...

Did her body *have* to respond with such unbridled delight
to the idea of so much stern, glowering disapproval locked
inside one hot man?

Maybe she liked Luke's steely self-control too much, Lucia

reflected, glancing at his poster image. It was certainly enough to overrule her fear of men.

Most men. Picking up her bag, she made a mental note to get the strap repaired. It had suffered a few injuries when she had used it to beat off the concierge. Teeth, nails, handbag, heel of her shoe… A frantic struggle which seemed so feeble now she looked back. But at least she had got away. Eventually.

The concierge had made her feel dirty, calling her names as she ran from the room, clutching her ripped shirt together. He'd said she was asking for it, when nothing could be further from the truth. She did like parties, and she liked flirting with hot guys, but now she could see that her fun-filled reputation had done her no favours. She could just imagine Luke's scorn if he ever found out what had happened. Getting changed in the staffroom without remembering to put the lock on the door? It was such a stupid thing to do. But she had to try to put it behind her or she would never get on with her life.

Tilting her chin, Lucia gave Luke's image one last confident stare, but the ache still remained. Where was he now? *With the blonde?* Perhaps Luke had sensed she was tainted—that the concierge had had his hands all over her. *Everywhere.* It made her stomach heave just thinking about it. She could still remember his fingers intimately feeling…squeezing… probing, and his sour breath choking her as she struggled to escape. If Luke knew that he would just think, *Party girl. What do you expect?*

She jumped as her phone rang, and then frowned as she checked the number. She had to take a moment before she could answer. Talk of the devil—though Luke would have no truck with hell. *What? No air-con?* Luke would be more likely to hold a season ticket to cloud extreme, where he could strum his whip beneath the glow of an oat-fed halo. No way would he waste his time on an aerodynamically inefficient tail and a totally useless pitchfork unless he could use it to strike a polo ball.

'Luke,' she said finally, when she had calmed down a little. 'What a nice surprise. Did you leave something at the club?'

'In the unlikely event I *had* left something at the club I would go back to pick it up. I wouldn't call you.'

Well. That told her. Luke couldn't have sounded less enthusiastic had he tried. Crouched on the bench seat, with her legs drawn up, she hugged the phone. 'Of course not,' she said, injecting energy into her voice. 'So, what can I do for you?'

'I didn't see you when I left the club. You were working, I expect.'

'I'm sorry. I—'

'Strange,' he rapped over her. 'The first time I saw you at the club you assured me you weren't working there often. But the manager says you are. And he knows you as Anita. What's going on, Lucia? Why are you lying to me?'

'What I do or don't do is none of your business, Luke.'

'Nacho made it my business.'

'So you're my brother's deputy now?'

'I'm your brother's friend,' Luke argued quietly.

Luke couldn't have disarmed her faster. There was no point starting a feud with someone Nacho loved when the very last thing she wanted was a total break with her family. 'So why are you calling me?'

'I'm concerned about you, Lucia.'

'Well, don't be. And if my brothers are so worried, why don't they call? Or are they too busy playing polo?'

'Why are you always so suspicious, Lucia?'

'Because you're all joined at the hip,' she flashed. 'And because my brothers never like me to have too long a leash. Isn't that right, Luke?'

There was silence at the other end of the line.

Damn him! Luke had made her feel homesick, reminding

her of all the warmth and support she received in Argentina. It made everything here seem bleaker—the wind rattling round the caravan, the freezing cold water, the hideous episode with the concierge which she was doing her best to block out, and then her subsequent high-speed drive through the night, reckless...

And her lousy job at the club.

A dead-end job to end all dead-end jobs.

Her heart sank like a stone. She couldn't bear for gorgeous, glorious, successful Luke to know her life was a complete and utter mess. And she certainly couldn't bear for him to share that little nugget of information with her brothers. If they knew what had happened... How they would blame her for her frivolous, careless party-girl lifestyle. She deserved this, didn't she?

Sucking in a deep, steadying breath, she said briskly, 'Is this a courtesy call, or does it have some purpose, Luke?' She needed him to get off the line fast, before her voice broke.

'I've never heard you in this mood before,' he said suspiciously.

'Independent, do you mean?' Her fingers had turned white on the phone. It was one thing acting tough, but when she really wanted to cling to Luke's disembodied presence like a brainless limpet until all the bad things went away it was far better to end the call as soon as she could.

'Are you still there, Lucia?'

'I'm here.'

Luke checking up on her was nothing new. She had been an object of amusement for Luke and her brothers for as long as Lucia could remember. They thought she was a fancy, frilly little joke—a novelty, a pet they would like to keep locked up in a box until they decided to bring her out and coo over her on those rare occasions when they weren't trying to murder each other on the polo field.

'Just tell my brothers everything's fine.'

'*Is* everything fine?' Luke repeated suspiciously. 'Maybe I should check that statement for myself.'

'If you've nothing better to do. You'll only make a wasted journey. I'm working all hours.'

'Is that so?' he said.

'I do take a break from partying sometimes.'

And now tears were backing up behind her eyes. She knew what Luke and her brothers thought of her. Flighty Lucia, they had used to call her, flapping their arms and laughing. What a joke that was. And of course little Lucia was always getting herself into trouble, always needing to be bailed out, they used to say, while one of them leaned his forearm on the top of her head. Well, not this time. She was none of those things now.

Steadying her voice, she said, 'You're actually quite lucky to catch me—'

'The club opens at eight in the morning?'

'Don't pretend you don't know about my second job. I saw you getting cosy with Van Rickter. I'm sure he told you everything you wanted to know.'

And what was Luke doing in Cornwall, having meetings with a man like Van Rickter? Lucia wondered. Was Luke going to buy the club? Her stomach sank. She knew nothing about Luke or his life, Lucia realised.

'Lucia?'

'I'm still here,' she confirmed.

She wished she could tell Luke about Margaret and how things were, talk things through with him. Luke had always had a clear head on his shoulders. But his tone was brisk and impersonal and didn't invite confidences.

'Where are you calling from?' Curling into a small defensive ball, she pictured him relaxing back somewhere warm and luxurious, with his feet up and a coffee to hand as he made this duty call.

'In transit. Why?'

'No reason.' She could hardly ask where he was in transit from or to without seeming unduly interested. 'You didn't tell me why you're in Cornwall...'

'Didn't I?'

'Do you have business with Van Rickter?' she pried. 'Are you calling me from the Grand?'

'So many questions, Lucia.' The first hint of amusement coloured Luke's voice. 'I'm not far away, as it happens.'

The blonde was probably having her nails done and Luke had nothing better to do than harass her, Lucia guessed, flashing a glare at his centrefold. If there was one thing guaranteed to switch her thoughts from her own screw-ups it was wondering how one of the sharpest men on the planet had been caught in such a picture *and* by a Technicolor blonde. She had never known Luke to let his guard down before.

'So, what do you do when you're not working, Lucia?' he said.

'Oh, you know...'

'That bad?'

'I'm usually so exhausted after work I just sleep.' True, unfortunately, but definitely the safest option.

'So you wouldn't want to come to supper with me tonight?'

'With you?' Luke couldn't have surprised her more. There were so many reasons why she wanted to go out with him, and so many reasons why she shouldn't.

'Why not?' he said, adding casually, 'It *is* your birthday, isn't it?'

Her brothers must have put him up to this, Lucia realised as her heart thundered a tattoo. 'Yes, it is,' she confirmed. Matching Luke for nonchalance, she added, 'Don't tell me you're asking me out on a date?'

'You wish,' he countered, with a flash of the camaraderie they had shared before hormones kicked in. 'Well?' he demanded in the same offhand tone. 'What's your answer?'

She had to release her stranglehold on the phone and shake her hand to get the blood flowing through her fingers again before she could think straight. If she accepted, and Luke started questioning her, how would she explain to him what one part freedom in Cornwall to nine parts humiliation in London felt like? How would he react when she told him that there wasn't a chance she was going to turn her back on her new life? How would she hide from Luke what had happened in London?

And what about the blonde?

No. She couldn't accept. If she went out with Luke it would be—

What? Surrender? Defeat? Weakness? *What?*

Wasn't she guilty of overreacting just a little bit?

While she was trying to decide Luke started talking 'horse'—a language spoken exclusively by Luke and her brothers. Dreams were almost always better than reality, Lucia reflected, gazing at Luke's centrefold, thinking maybe she owed it to the Sisterhood to warn the women of the world about him. Luke's poster image suggested an impossibly sexual animal with a body designed for sin, when she knew the only type of physical activity that really got Luke's juices flowing involved a bit, a bridle and a pair of really sharp spurs.

'Well, if everything's okay your end, Lucia?'

'What?' She realised he was about to sign off. 'Don't go yet—I mean… It's um…fun talking to a dinosaur.' She laughed, hoping Luke hadn't detected the flash of desperation in her voice. No one said she had to go cold turkey. A familiar voice was like tonic wine. You drank it down and then you felt better. Right?

'*Now* you want to talk?' he said dryly. 'How about you start with what really brought you back to Cornwall? And for goodness' sake call your brothers, will you?'

'I have.' *So many times.* But they were *always* playing polo. And as for Cornwall... 'I'm just taking a break in Cornwall.'

No way was she telling Luke the truth. It would be the easiest thing in the world to howl down the phone that things hadn't turned out the way she'd hoped they would, and could Luke please lend her the money to fly home? But if she did that this climb-back of hers would be over before it had started, and she would have proved everyone right about her. Deep inside she would hate herself. She would be a failure and everyone would know it.

'Well, I hope everything works out for you, Lucia—'

'Tonight,' she cut in with one final burst of desperate lonely energy. 'That supper you mentioned?'

When this was met by an ominous silence she realised Luke had probably had second thoughts. Maybe it was time to eat some humble pie.

'I think I could make it tonight.'

'So you have no plans?' he said flatly. And when she remained silent he added, 'I never thought I'd see the day when Lucia Acosta stayed home on her birthday... But if it's a matter of money and you'd rather go out with some friends—'

'Stop that, Luke!' Money was the way her brothers had always controlled her.

'Don't be so touchy,' he fired back.

'Then get it through your head that I don't need your money. I've got everything I need right here.'

She had birthday gifts from her friends, and a few clothes if she wanted a night out. Well, she had the sale rail spectacular she'd snatched from her room before bolting from the hotel in London, together with some shoes she'd had repaired. She hadn't stopped to pack a case. She couldn't have spent a second longer than she had to in the hotel while her body was crawling with invisible insects where the concierge's hands had touched her.

'It seems you've got everything covered,' Luke was saying, while she shrank like Alice to the size of a pea. 'I'll get off your case, Lucia. I was only trying to look out for you.'

She hugged herself tighter, waiting for the line to be cut, for the silence to grow and gather. But Luke didn't cut the line.

'Are you really spending your birthday on your own?' he drawled, in a mock-weary tone.

'For goodness' sake, stop going on about it,' she flashed. 'I don't need a cake and candles at my age. I'm a big girl now.'

'Good. Then you can have supper with me at the Grand. Eight o' clock sharp. And, Lucia?'

'Yes?'

'Don't be late.'

The *Grand*? She had been to the elegant hotel many times with her parents, and the entire family had always dressed up for the occasion. She had nothing remotely suitable for an evening at the Grand in her sparse arsenal of clothes.

So was she going to turn down Luke's invitation? A warm room, a decent meal, the company of an old friend...

Her stomach growled in anticipation of its first proper meal in a long time that didn't include scones, cream and jam, fries or hot chocolate. 'Don't worry, Luke. I won't be la—'

Luke had cut the line.

What on earth had she agreed to? The Grand was one of those seriously exclusive hotels that attracted seriously exclusive guests. And if she was going to brave it in her sale rail spectacular, did she *really* want to prove the fact that sun-starved olive skin looked no better than sun-starved pale white skin?

Lucia's gaze strayed to the well-past-its-sell-by-date bottle of fake tan on the shelf, which had been there when she'd moved in. She had to do something to make herself feel better. She couldn't possibly look any worse than she did now, she reasoned, reaching for it.

CHAPTER FIVE

Get a Tan

You will have noticed that The Tan was actually item number four on my to-do list, appearing after item number three: The Wax. I think you'll agree that's proof positive that the list was written by my fourteen-year-old-self long before the ramifications of turning fuzzy black leg hair a strange shade of green with the overuse of chemicals had actually occurred to me.

You will also know that a fake tan takes time to develop—something else I had yet to learn. With my olive skin I was naturally sun-kissed in Argentina, thanks to the lovely weather, and even when I was at school in England there were always half-term holidays and trips home, so I was a bit of a fake-tan virgin. When one application didn't seem to work I applied another... and another...figuring that since it was past its sell-by date maybe it wasn't as strong as normal.

I couldn't have been more wrong.

I decided to wear my sale rail spectacular for the birthday supper with Luke. It's a strappy dress in electric blue with a huge wilted rose dotted with shocking pink diamanté pinned at the front, which was probably the reason the dress hadn't sold. Removing the brooch made a whole world of difference.

What surprised me most of all was that after work-ing such long hours, and skipping a few meals due to lack of time and money, I had lost a few of my comfort-food pounds. In fact the dress almost fitted me. But, as previously mentioned, those long hours spent indoors had done my olive skin no favours, so the success of the night hung on a bottle of Tanfastic Your World.

YES, he had spoken to Nacho. Inviting Lucia for supper was his good deed for the day—make that the year.

'Would you spoil Lucia a bit?' Nacho had asked him, no doubt overcome with relief that Luke had tracked down his missing sister.

'I'll buy her supper,' Luke had offered.

'And a card?' Nacho prompted.

He exhaled steadily before answering. 'I'll see what the hotel shop can offer.'

'Thanks, Luke.'

Nacho's gratitude made him feel guilty, and then he de-tected another question in Nacho's voice. 'You want me to try and buy her a little gift or something?' he said, anticipating Nacho's next request.

'Please,' Nacho said with relief. 'I'll wire you the money—'

'*Dios*, Nacho,' Luke exclaimed, slipping into the lingo they customarily used. 'It will all wash through—and I won't find much in a hotel shop.'

'Just do your best, Luke.'

He shrugged, reasoning he could throw money at it—though what a wild child with a penchant for scrubbing floors might want for her birthday escaped him.

Oh, this was nerve-racking. Her hand was actually shaking. She'd never used to be completely useless when it came to men. Quite the opposite, in fact. It had used to come naturally to her—she'd never had to think about it before. Flirting with hot guys, knowing they wanted her, and always, always being in control. But now it was different. She had had a king-sized setback that had spiralled completely out of control, but she was determined not to let it colour her whole life. It was just that going out for supper with a guy she'd had a crush on for what seemed for ever, who looked like a sex god and who probably looked on her as a nuisance at best—well, that took a lot of preparation.

The dress wasn't bad on reflection. It was certainly colourful. *Retro*, she corrected herself, trying to imagine how her former self would have pulled it off. Surely it was just about confidence? If she felt confident she could make it work. *If she felt confident…*

Who was she kidding? Lucia thought, blinking back tears as she tried to put her lenses in. Oh, bother them—she'd just have to wear glasses.

She parked around the back at the Grand, easing her ancient car into a gap between a sleek black limousine and a gleaming off-roader she doubted had ever seen a field. Well—deep breath—this was it.

She marched along the gravel path, dipping once to adjust the heel strap on her stratospheric sandals. That brief swoop was enough to shoot rain from her collar down the Grand Canyon between her breasts. She didn't have a raincoat smart enough to wear to the Grand to protect her from the elements, so she was wearing the luminous yellow sou'wester Margaret had loaned her for heavy work outside. With nothing to cover her head apart from a handbag, it was probably safe to say her make-up had washed off and her hair was a mat of black frizz.

The doorman ignored her. How could he not see the plump girl in luminous yellow oilcloth with a handbag balanced on her head?

Oh, well.

'Lucia.'

'Luke…' She gazed at the vision in designer jeans, a crisp white shirt and tailored jacket, standing at the open door. 'Amazing,' she breathed, squinting at him through her rain-speckled glasses.

'Are you coming in?' Luke said briskly. 'Or am I supposed to stand here all night?'

The uniformed doorman took the hint and hurried out of his regular position to take control of the door. 'My apologies, sir,' he said effusively, while Lucia blinked owlishly at the two men.

Luke linked her arm through his as if he had been waiting for this moment all his life. 'How good to see you,' he added warmly.

As Luke led her away she glanced behind her and had the satisfaction of seeing astonishment colour the doorman's face. She thought about sticking her tongue out, and then thought better of it when Luke cautioned her, 'No!' reading her with his usual ease.

Luke escorted her to the cloakroom, where he helped her with the sou'wester. 'At least you're dry underneath,' he said, ignoring the surprised look of the pretty girl behind the desk, who couldn't seem to take her eyes off Lucia as Luke handed her oilskin cover. 'Your ticket,' he said. 'Put it in your bag before you lose it,' he prompted.

Lucia was incapable of speech. She had just caught sight of herself in the ornate gilt mirror. Now she knew why the girl was staring. Her make-up was smudged, which was only to be expected after braving a rainstorm, and her hair could not have been bushier—but what she couldn't have anticipated were the tiger stripes of orange and olive where the fake tan had washed off. It was not a good look.

'Would you like to go and freshen up before we go in to

supper?' Luke suggested. Reaching into his pocket, he pulled out a clean white handkerchief and handed it to her discreetly.

Nothing would help. Her evening was ruined. Her hair was having an electrical storm and her skin-tight dress was totally unsuitable for a cold night in a posh hotel. Nothing had changed at the Grand, and as Lucia had expected every other woman there had chosen to wear outfits best described as classic and timeless. Certainly they were discreet. No one was wearing anything to compete with Lucia's electric blue Lycra number and the fake tan dripping down her arms. 'I'm so sorry, Luke.'

'What are you sorry about?' he said. Linking her arm through his again, he steered her across the lobby in the direction of the ladies' restroom. 'Go wash up. You'll be fine.'

'I'm so embarrassed...'

'Lucia,' he said firmly, 'you're not going to let a little bit of slapdash painting spoil your birthday, are you?'

A smile was hovering around Luke's sexy lips—that sexy mouth was something she must put out of her mind immediately. She had enough on her hands, concentrating on disaster management.

The disaster was too extreme, Lucia concluded. Fear of men, fear of Luke finding out what had happened in London, and now this. 'Seriously, Luke—I'd rather go home. Even if the fake tan does wash off, I'm not dressed for this.'

'It's your birthday,' he said, as if that made any fashion *faux pas* acceptable. 'I'll wait out here. Take your time, but make a thorough job of it,' he added with a crooked grin.

She could just imagine Luke's report to her brothers— *Lucia was fine the last time I saw her, if a bit liverish.*

Going into the restroom, she planted her fists on the side of the basin. She couldn't even bear to look at herself in the mirror she was such a mess. Finally, pulling herself together, she ran the taps. She was going to scrub and scrub until her skin was clean again—until she really felt clean again. And then she was going to man up and join Luke for supper as if what had happened was a regular part of any date.

'I'm sorry,' she said wryly as she exited the restroom. 'I couldn't save your hanky.'

Luke's lips curved in the same attractive grin. 'I've got plenty more.'

She gasped as he leaned forward. 'Oh,' she murmured as he removed her glasses and stood back to take a really good look at her.

'Wow...'

'Wow, good? Or wow, bad?' she said tensely.

'Wow, pretty damn fantastic,' Luke murmured.

Nodding to the *maître d'*, Luke linked her arm through his and led her into the glittering crystal and gilt dining room, where it soon became obvious that no one gave a damn what she looked like because everyone was staring at Luke. Waving the waiter away, he insisted on pulling out her chair.

'What's this?' she asked, staring at the envelope on her plate.

'Damn, that looks like an envelope to me.' Reaching across the table, Luke put his big paw over hers. 'Before you open it, can I just say you look amazing tonight, Lucia?'

'And you couldn't have been more surprised?' she supplied in a comic voice.

Luke shook his head as if he gave up. As he called the wine waiter over Lucia wondered if she had freed him from the obligation to work his way through the list of appropriate compliments her brothers must have foisted on him.

'Your best champagne, please,' Luke requested as the waiter hovered. 'Well?' he prompted, turning back to her. 'Aren't you going to open the card?'

'Of course.' She stopped as Luke reached beneath his

chair and produced a gift-wrapped present. 'You really didn't need to.'

'Just open it,' he said.

He felt guilty as Lucia's eyes lit with surprise and pleasure. He'd spent so much time teasing her over the years he had never really thought about Lucia's feelings. *He* didn't have any—why should she? But Lucia had enough feelings for both of them, he realised as she stared down at the gift. Her surprised expression touched him somewhere deep.

'Don't get too excited,' he warned. 'It's just something I picked up at the hotel shop.' *On the instigation of your brother*, he silently added. But this was the first time he'd bought Lucia anything. If he had even looked at her the wrong way when they were younger Lucia's brothers would have ripped his head off.

She opened the card first. He was sorry he hadn't been able to go somewhere with a wider selection—get something with a funny message on the front, something more appropriate for Lucia. The card was nice enough, but it was one of those 'suits every occasion' blank cards that hotels stocked. There were a bunch of flowers on the front in no-nonsense bright colours.

'Lovely,' she said, reading what he'd written inside: *To my old sparring partner—Happy Birthday, Luke.* 'No one could accuse you of forgetting the old days.' She smiled, as if that pleased her, and then turned the card over to read the script on the back. 'Anemones are for unfading love, hmm?' Her eyes were sparkling with humour as they searched his. 'I'm betting you didn't think to read the back?'

'You'd be right,' he admitted gruffly, caught out redhanded.

'Anyway, it's very nice of you to buy me a card at all, so thank you.'

'Aren't you going to open your present?' She was still touching the card with her fingertip, as if there was something meaningful to be gleaned from his bold black writing. 'Go on—open it,' he pressed. Was he getting into this?

'Luke, you shouldn't have.'

'And risk you having a strop because I hadn't got you anything?'

'I'm not fourteen any more, Luke.'

He'd reminded her of her fourteenth birthday party, which Nacho had arranged. It had been heavily policed by her brothers, who had checked up on Lucia and her friends every five minutes. Predictably, the girls had swooned when the boys had walked in, while Lucia had only craved a single glance from Luke. But the older they'd got, the more Luke had pushed her away. She had bumped into him the next day in the hay barn and screamed at him that he hadn't even wished her a happy birthday, let alone bought her a present.

'I've never made your life easy, have I, Luke?'

'At least we're on the same page where that's concerned,' he agreed.

He had bought a shawl—soft and feminine in moss-green cashmere. He'd thought it would look great against Lucia's hair and eyes—though, admittedly, it wouldn't look quite so great with a bright blue dress. 'If you'd rather change it for another colour...'

'I wouldn't dream of it,' she said, holding it to her face. 'My brothers generally buy me pieces of tack for my pony.'

When all the teenage Lucia had craved was the latest colour lipstick, or music by whatever group was in vogue, he guessed.

'I loved it that they remembered my birthday,' she went on, 'but sometimes...'

Sometimes she'd missed her mother, he silently supplied.

Closing her eyes, Lucia rested her cheek against the shawl.

'Good,' he said briskly, jerking them both out of the spell she had woven. 'Job done. Shall we order? Are you hungry?'

'Starving,' she admitted. Her cheeks fired red. 'I mean—'

'We're here to eat, Lucia,' he pointed out.

Calling the waiter over, he ordered plenty, in case Lucia didn't order enough, and when the food arrived she ate with such relish it was hard to keep up. Lucia wasn't just hungry, she was ravenous.

He tried not to dwell on this, but as she scraped up the last of the Crème Anglaise from her plate and sighed with pleasure he couldn't hold back any longer. 'When did you last eat?'

'It's been a long time since I've eaten anything this good,' she admitted, laying down her spoon.

'Is that it?' he pressed.

'Lunchtime,' she said defensively, sitting up straight. 'One of Margaret's delicious cream teas.'

He made no comment. 'Okay, so now you're fed and watered, how about coming clean about why you're working at the club?'

'It's a job, Luke.'

'Has Van Rickter been bullying you?'

'What is this? The Spanish Inquisition?'

'*Has* Van Rickter been bullying you?' he repeated, holding her flickering gaze.

'Of course he hasn't. I feel sorry for him, really. He's such a frustrated individual—not *that* way,' she said quickly, her cheeks colouring. 'Are we going to have coffee now?'

He recognised the diversionary tactic, but was more determined than ever to get to the bottom of whatever Lucia was holding back. He was close to certain that there was a man involved. He dangled some bait. 'Nacho was telling me about the hotel management job you had in London.'

'I'm taking a sabbatical,' she said quickly.

Which made no sense to him.

A fork hit the floor. It wasn't one of Lucia's better ruses. As she bent to retrieve it he waved the waiter away.

With her face hidden by the linen folds of the tablecloth,

she was trying to buy time in the hope that thoughts of what had happened in London might fade.

'Lucia?'

She exhaled with frustration, seeing that Luke had joined her under the table, his face level with hers. 'What are you doing?' she asked impatiently.

'I might ask you the same question. And we can't stay down here for ever—people will talk.'

As if Luke would care. Straightening up, she handed the fork to the waiter with an apology.

Luke remained silent until the man had gone, and then asked, 'Are you okay, Lucia?'

'I dropped a fork, Luke.'

'So you didn't have to answer any more questions about London, I presume?'

Luke's expression was one she recognised: unwavering and disbelieving. Which said he was prepared to hang in for however long it took to get at the truth. He proved this theory with his next question. 'So, what did you learn in London?'

'Plenty.'

'Such as?' he probed.

That the world without family was a hostile, angry place, and that all men didn't behave with the same chivalry towards women as Luke and her brothers. She might resent their interference in her life, but she had never realised that honour was in such short supply before.

She almost choked on her relief as their coffee arrived and there was the usual interruption as the waiters set everything out in front of them. Luke pushed a dish of chocolates over to her side of the table without another word.

Lucia devoured the chocolates as she had devoured everything else within reach, with a freakish type of nervous energy—as if she were a squirrel storing up for winter. Whatever she was hiding from him it was big. The impulse to transfer money into her account ASAP so she could buy some proper food was banging in his head, but he could just imagine Lucia's reaction if he tried. And something told him that a balanced diet was the least of her problems. But he could hope.

'Are you eating properly?'

'I eat too much.' She grimaced.

A diet of cream teas and chocolate, if he remembered Margaret's specialities correctly. And he wouldn't be surprised if any money Lucia saved from her earnings went to help Margaret out rather than any payment flowing the other way. Lucia had always had a generous heart. Too generous sometimes.

'Great music,' she said, drawing his attention to the Salsa band.

'They must have known you were coming,' he said, remembering Lucia on the dance floor at her brother's wedding. Recollections of that evening curled heat around him. 'Would you like to dance?'

'Oh, no, that's okay,' she said, pulling back in her chair.

'I wouldn't want to embarrass you with my skill,' he agreed.

She relaxed. 'Your *skill*?' One brow rose. 'Since when have polo players had any skill to speak of—unless they are mounted on a really great horse?'

'Ouch.'

'I've had the chance to practise that one,' she admitted, with a wry spark from the old days in her look.

'A few times, I imagine,' he agreed. 'Shall we?' he said, standing up.

Her lips pressed down as she stared at his outstretched hand. 'I suppose one dance won't kill me.'

As he held her chair he felt a surge of anticipation at the thought of holding Lucia in his arms that had absolutely no connection with doing a favour for her brother.

CHAPTER SIX

The first step is the hardest. And after that it's all downhill, right?

Not this time, because tonight when Luke took my hand and led me onto the dance floor the bad thoughts took flight and all I could see in my mind's eye was Luke riding flat out across the sand. Riding bareback, barechested, wearing the designer jeans his mother always insisted her staff must put a crease down the front of. Luke wore them cut off and frayed, covered in hoof oil and wet with sea spray, so that they clung to his hard-muscled thighs.

He'd whoop as he overtook the last of my brothers, leaving them roaring with frustration in his wake, lying flat on his horse's neck, encouraging it to go even faster. Wings of diamond-studded mist would spread out behind him as if he were riding Pegasus and they might take to the sky at any moment.

At least that was what I always imagined when I was fourteen, as I sat watching him from the shadows by the rock pool.

As THEY threaded their way through the tables Luke's warm palm in the hollow of her back was a badly needed wake-up call. Luke could read her like a book, so she had to cage all her wild, unfounded, fearful thoughts and place all imaginings about a romance with Luke in the never-going-to-happen box.

'Are you cold?' he asked with concern as she shivered with a whole mix of emotions when he gathered her in.

'Just frightened for my feet,' she managed dryly.

'Don't be,' Luke murmured.

She needn't have worried. Once they reached the dance floor Luke's touch was light and impersonal, and he was careful to keep a space between them that would have made a maiden aunt feel safe.

He loved Salsa dancing. He loved the rhythm and the music and the contact—especially tonight, with Lucia moving so easily in his arms. Dance was liberating, and a great prelude to sex. Though not with Lucia, of course. He held her well away from him. But she moved so easily it wasn't long before his mind strayed onto the dark side. Dance was like sex. Trust had to be established and then limits set. Timing was all-important too.

His appetite sharpened when Lucia, having grown so much in confidence during the dance that she was almost back to the girl he knew, escaped him to execute a few hot Salsa moves of her own. Other men were watching her, and he found he didn't like that. And when she yipped, *'Ay, caramba,'* laughing as she threw her head back so her luscious hair swept the full curve of her buttocks, he knew he was in for trouble. He could have watched her all night. Private viewing would be his preference…

Most men looked awkward on the dance floor, but Luke was so well coordinated he looked hot, and they moved well together.

'You're a great dancer, Lucia.'

'For such a great hulking oaf, you're not so bad yourself.' And if she couldn't take the heat on the dance floor there were plenty of women watching Luke who could, Lucia concluded.

'We fit so well together,' he said, drawing her close.

So much of her was glued to Luke it was hard to disagree, but telling herself that Luke would never hurt her, or take advantage of her, didn't help her heart to slow down. Again, she was worrying unnecessarily, for when the music stopped Luke escorted her back to the table.

'That was so good!' she exclaimed as he pulled her chair out, feeling as if everything bad that had happened in London must have floated away.

'Will you excuse me, please, Lucia?' Luke asked once she was seated.

'Had enough of me?' she teased, angling her chin in enquiry.

Dipping his head, he murmured in her ear, 'There's something I must do. I'll be back in a couple of minutes.'

She glanced around as Luke left the restaurant, and noticed that every other woman was doing the same thing. Picking up her champagne glass, she gave a wry smile to think of so much man going to waste on her. She was about to take a sip of the sparkling wine when a man lost his balance and lurched into her table.

'I'm afraid that seat's taken,' she explained politely.

Her stomach clenched with alarm when the man ignored her and insisted on trying to sit down. He was so drunk he could barely stand, she realised. She glanced around, looking for help, but all the other diners were eating or chatting, and the waiters were busy.

It occurred to her then that before her experience with the concierge she could have handled something like this without missing a beat, but her brain seemed to have been rewired along with her confidence levels, and all she could force out of her mouth was a weak 'Please don't do that.'

The drunk ignored her.

It all seemed to be spinning out of control, just like the

day in London when the concierge had locked them both in
the staffroom. Her chest felt tight. She couldn't breathe. And
though a part of her brain said all this situation required was
some firm action on her part she remained in a bubble of apprehension, waiting for the inevitable touch, the pinch, the
grope.

Lurching forward, the drunk made a hideous munching
sound as he reached for her breasts. In terror, she jerked back,
and her drink flew everywhere as she rocked sideways off
her chair.

Strong hands caught hold of her before she could fall to
the floor. 'Are you okay?' Luke demanded in a shocked tone.

For a moment she could only stare at him in blank surprise,
but then she slowly became aware that other people had gathered round and were staring at her with concern.

'Did he hurt you, Lucia?' Luke asked in a low, fierce voice.

'No… No, I don't think so.' Luke was holding her hands
so tightly they'd turned white. She realised she was gasping
for breath like a landed fish. 'I feel such a fool.'

'Don't.' Shielding her from the onlookers with the bulk of
his body, Luke lifted her out of the chair.

'Where are you taking me?'

'Questions later,' he insisted, leading her out of the restaurant with one strong arm locked around her shoulders as he
drew her into his body to keep her safe.

She glanced behind them. 'My shawl!'

The *maitre d'* handed it to Luke. Having thanked him, Luke
asked for a bottle of good cognac to be sent up to his suite.

'Right away, sir. We're very sorry, sir. We'll take care of it
right away.' The *maitre d'* hurried away.

'I can't believe I only left you for a couple of minutes and
someone tried to spoil your birthday,' Luke grated out as he
stabbed the elevator button.

Luke's eyes were full of concern when he turned to search

her face. She had really blown it now. 'Nothing could spoil my birthday.' Nothing except her weak, pathetic, shaking voice—which was more proof, should he need it, that something dreadful must have happened to turn the sexy, confident, party-girl Luke had used to know into the woman he held in his arms right now.

Needless to say, he picked up on it right away.

'Is this the girl who could stand up to four fierce brothers?' he demanded tensely. 'What has happened to you, Lucia? What happened in London?'

'Nothing,' she insisted, shivering as the elevator doors slid closed, enclosing them in the small cabin. Surely it couldn't contain so much emotion?

'Nothing?' Luke murmured, his gaze sharpening on her face. 'Why can't you trust me with the truth, Lucia? Haven't we known each other long enough?'

The tension between them increased as the lift soared up to the penthouse floor, where she stepped out with relief into a beautifully decorated hallway. A lovely fresh smell hit her immediately, and though she was still reeling from her experience in the dining room she could appreciate the muted décor. Ivory walls and a thick crimson carpet beneath her feet to muffle sound, gilt mirrors glittering beneath concealed lighting. There were prints on the wall, and decorative touches of ruby and gold on lampshades and drapes.

Warm colours to make the guests feel cosy, she supposed as Luke opened the door leading into his suite. But she was still shivering.

Luke had barely closed the door when there was a discreet tap on it. It was two waiters arriving with coffee and brandy, and there was a birthday cake on a tray.

'So that's what you were arranging for me,' she said, touched by the gesture.

Luke tipped the waiters and hustled them out.

'You're spoiling me,' she said as he poured her a brandy and insisted she take a sip.

'I refuse to be distracted, Lucia,' Luke assured her. 'Ever since I saw you at the club I've known something was wrong. And now tonight—'

'There's nothing wrong,' she interrupted. 'It's just that you've never seen me striking out on my own before. It's been a lovely evening. Can't we leave it at that?'

'A *lovely* evening?' Luke queried with a penetrating glance.

'So a drunk spoiled it briefly?' She shrugged, brushing it off. 'I can't explain why I overreacted. I'm tired. It must be because I'm tired. It's not as if I haven't seen a drunk before.' She laughed, but Luke's face remained watchful and unsmiling. 'Thank you for the shawl,' she added, stroking it as the tension between them mounted. 'I don't know when I've enjoyed a birthday more.'

'Possibly the day you celebrated by putting burrs under my saddle?' Luke suggested, but there was little humour in his voice, and his stare plumbed deep as he searched for the truth she refused to share with him.

'That was a contender,' she agreed, forcing out another laugh.

They drank their coffee in tense silence, leaving the cake untouched, and finally Luke stood up. 'I'll take you home,' he said.

And let him see where she was living? Wouldn't that be the perfect end to the perfect day?

'You don't need to. My car's parked right outside.'

'You've had a shock, and I won't let you go home alone,' Luke said flatly.

'Luke, I don't need a babysitter.'

'You've had a drink. I haven't,' he said, glancing at her empty brandy glass.

'Then I'll ask them to call a cab. Look, I don't want us to part like this.'

'Like what? You're the one holding back, Lucia.'

'Why are you so suspicious? You and my brothers are all the same.' Composing herself, she stood to face him. 'Thank you for a wonderful evening, Luke—for the meal, the gift, the card, the cake. You're very kind—'

'I *am* very kind.'

She longed to cling to that grain of humour, so she could remember how it used to be between them before she felt grubby and Luke became so far removed. She was almost at the door when she stopped and impulsively, almost as if she had to prove something to herself, stood on tiptoe to plant a kiss on Luke's stubble-blackened jaw. 'Thank you for everything, Luke.'

Luke turned to look at her at just the wrong moment—or maybe it was the right moment. Whatever happened, their lips touched briefly.

He might as well have plugged her in to the socket in the wall. She drew a shocked breath as the charge flashed through her. And, most confusing of all, it wasn't fear that held her motionless in front of him but some shadow of the girl she'd used to be. It was enough.

Instead of moving away, Luke laced his fingers through her hair and drew her closer still. 'Happy birthday, Lucia,' he murmured, repeating the shock treatment in a more leisurely fashion.

She had to tell herself that Luke was just being kind—that this was a reaction to what had happened to her with the drunk, and not some declaration of intent on his part to take things further. But it was like a dream. Only better than any dream she'd ever had.

'There's something you need to know, Lucia,' Luke said rather formally, pulling back. 'We're not kids any more and I don't think of myself as your babysitter. One more thing,' he added, catching hold of her arm when, thoroughly confused by now, she went to move away. 'If you play with fire you *will* get burned.'

With her nerves stretched as taut as a bow string, she almost laughed. Luke had no idea how true that was.

He saw something in her face that made him drag her back. And there was no mistake this time. This kiss was no accident. Luke's lips were firm and persuasively mobile, and when he held her it was with both hands resting lightly either side of her ribcage, so that his thumbs could tease the full swell of her breasts.

But as the warm wave of pleasure swept over her, driving everything bad away, he let her go. 'I'm taking you home,' he said abruptly, turning for the door.

Even after all this time she received the message loud and clear. Luke was a warrior, with a warrior's appetite, and no one should mess with that. And as a friend he was hurt that she couldn't bring herself to confide in him. It was a dangerous combination.

This time she didn't stop to argue, she just grabbed her coat.

The tension between them remained high as they drove back to the caravan park, where it developed into a full-scale snarling match about where Luke should drop her off.

'Do you seriously think I'm going to let you walk through the dark on your own?' he roared, slamming on the brakes.

'Don't you get it? I'm on my own now, and I'm fine,' she whipped back as Luke swung round to glare at her.

'I'm fine,' he mocked, in a whiney approximation of a girly voice, which made her want to launch herself at him and punch him like the old days.

But Luke was right about one thing. Those days were long gone.

'How do you think I've managed without you all this time?'

she demanded, when Luke remained tensely silent, with the steering wheel clenched in his big hands as if he'd like to rip it out of its fixings. 'Anyway, I'm getting out.'

There was still no response from Luke. And now there seemed to be a problem with the door, which rather spoiled her grand flounce off. 'Child lock, Luke?'

'If the shoe fits, Lucia.' His eyes had darkened to jet.

'Let me out right now,' she warned as he sat back, clearly not prepared to let her go. 'You can watch me as I walk to the caravan.'

'Oh, that's so kind of you,' Luke remarked sharply, reaching forward to release the locks.

The air was charged with tension, and Luke had made no mention of seeing her again. She sure as hell wasn't going to ask him. But there was a little pocket of guilt inside her that said, *Don't let the evening end like this. You'll never forgive yourself.*

She turned before stepping down. 'Thank you again for—'

'It was nothing,' he interrupted coldly.

'Well, thank you anyway.'

Luke sat immobile with his eyes narrowed on some distant horizon where she couldn't reach him. She felt wretched leaving like this. Her birthday night had been crammed with emotion and drama, which Luke had cruised through. He'd bought her a lovely gift and a card—even if at the instigation of her brother. And he had kissed her. *Luke had kissed her.* Her lips were still swollen.

Darting forward impulsively, she pressed a kiss on his stubble-roughened cheek. 'Thank you.'

'For goodness' sake, go,' he snapped, staring fixedly ahead.

He watched Lucia totter across the rutted field in her totally unsuitable shoes and her flapping yellow rubberised coat. How anyone could look quite so desirable in that get-up beat him.

But when he'd danced with her, when he'd held her, when he'd felt how warm and young and supple she was...how vulnerable... *When those full breasts had rubbed insistently against his chest.* How he hadn't dragged her to him and kissed the breath out of her lungs, he had no idea.

Raking his hair with frustration, he switched on the engine. Bang went the 'like a sister' theory. The urge to bury his face in Lucia's chest and hear her whimper with pleasure while he made love to her had almost overtaken him. It had even crossed his mind to have her in the car. With her feet up on the dash and endless adjustments available to the seats anything was possible.

Except that. Throwing the off-roader into reverse, he knew he would never throw away years of caring about Lucia for a mindless screw in a field. However much she tried his patience he would always be there for her. He had tried to blank her from his mind—goodness knows how hard he'd tried—but she never left his thoughts. She had her own little space in there.

Not so little, Luke accepted as he swung the wheel and turned the car onto the road. Kissing Lucia had been a revelation and had left him wanting more. Much more. What he needed now was distance from Lucia and a chance to put his thoughts in order so he could work out what had really happened tonight.

He made it half a mile down the road before standing on the brake. He could solve most problems with money, but not Lucia. And he couldn't trust anyone else to sort things out for her. No wonder she hadn't wanted him to see the state of the caravan she was living in. Maybe she did have something to prove—but not at the expense of her safety. Throwing the gear into reverse, he headed back.

This had nothing to do with her breasts, he told himself firmly as a mental image of his big calloused hands encompassing Lucia's lush breasts almost caused him to steer into a ditch. *Concentrate*, he told himself firmly as he tickled the brake pedal at the approach to the Sundowner Guest House and Holiday Park.

St Oswalds had suffered in the recession. This was something he knew a lot about, having rescued his family's business in a recession before going on to build his own company. Fortunately he had both the means and the practical capability to revive the village he believed in. Those childhood summer holidays were as clear in his mind now as they had ever been. So, however small a project the Sundowner might seem to anyone else, it was worth a king's ransom to him for the memories alone.

He could see a dim light shining in Lucia's decrepit van. Cursing softly as an image of a naked Lucia, wet and beneath a shower, flashed into his mind, he turned off the road and drove through rotting gates hanging off their hinges. This was worse than he had imagined. Everything was overgrown and desolate. Lucia's was the only van on what had once been a well-ordered pitch full of caravans. How could she continue to live here?

With his incredulity stretched to the limit for a moment, he could only think of barging in and dragging her out—but then reason kicked in. Lucia wanted responsibility, something he'd been loaded with at an early age. It hadn't done him any harm. Perhaps he should keep a watching brief and leave her to it.

He could do something here, Luke realised as his mind turned to practical matters. Energy flashed through him as ideas crowded his brain. He was eager to begin restoring the guest house to its former glory, but first he had to make sure Lucia was safe.

Switching off the lights, he freewheeled down the track. Halting behind some trees, he climbed out. Closing the door with barely a click, he walked up to Lucia's caravan and walked round it, examining it with the light from his mobile phone. There wasn't a lot he could do in the dark without tools, but he could improvise. He found rocks to place behind the wheels to act as chocks and, knocking the dirt off his hands, decided that, whether Lucia thanked him for his interference or not, he would definitely be back in the daylight to check everything out properly.

So this has nothing to do with sexual hunger and a desire to see Lucia again?

Not much, he mused wryly.

Staring round, he let his restless gaze linger on the moonlit beach and dramatic cliff line. Everything he could see increased his determination to do something to help the village that had once meant so much to him. It would take money and time, but...

Money he had in plenty. But time?

Maybe he could spare a few more days if Margaret agreed to his plan. He had a team of men who could turn around a place like this in no time flat. And when he went back he could steer the project from a distance, no problem, which would give him some much needed space from Lucia.

Lucia...

His concerns for her were back with a vengeance. Lucia lived in great comfort with her brothers in Argentina, so there had to be a very good reason for what she was doing here. Breaking free of four brothers he could understand, but hiding away in a tumbledown caravan out of season when there was no proper work to be had...

Her reaction to the drunk tonight had made it seem that Lucia was frightened of men, but Lucia, of all the women he knew, could handle men with both hands tied behind her back. There weren't many men as fierce as her brothers. Something didn't fit. He was going to hold that next call to Nacho until he'd made his own enquiries.

* * *

She woke the next morning, feeling something wasn't quite right. Then her brain kicked into gear and she buried her hot face in the pillow as the whole wonderful, terrible evening with Luke played out in her head. The last thing she wanted was Luke alerting her brothers to a problem. Or, worse, Luke riding in on his white charger to save her and sweeping her away. This was something she had to do alone.

As the phone trilled she tossed the pillow aside and made a lunge for it, then pulled a worried face when she recognised the number. 'Luke. I was about to ring to say thank you for last night.'

'So I beat you to it,' he said, in the low, husky voice that could always make her toes curl. 'No big deal. I take it you've just woken up?'

'How did you guess?' she said carefully, testing her still swollen lips with the tip of her tongue. 'Last night was wonderful, Luke.' She held her breath.

There was a pause, then Luke said with matching restraint, 'My pleasure, Lucia.'

'So,' she said, sitting up and raking her hair into some semblance of order, as if her brain cells might oblige and follow suit, 'what can I do for you, Luke?'

'Put the kettle on?'

'I'm sorry?'

'Put some clothes on too.'

'That's a little high-handed of you. This is my one morning off. What's the rush?'

'You might want to take a look outside.'

Wiping the condensation off the window with her sleeve, she felt her heart go into flight mode—though she gave a theatrical groan for Luke's benefit. 'Couldn't you sleep?' He was sitting outside in his vehicle.

'Not as well as you, clearly,' Luke said dryly.

Luke's voice sounded so close to her ear a blast of heat spiralled through her at the thought of his touch…his kiss…

Forget all that. Luke arriving in daylight, seeing how she was living, was the last thing she wanted. He couldn't know that she was going to clear a room for herself at the guest house just as soon as she'd sorted something nice out for Margaret. This was only the start of her new life and she couldn't risk Luke interfering.

'Aren't you going to invite me in, Lucia? Much as I love sitting out here in the rain…'

'Hang on. I'll just operate the electric gates.'

She could imagine Luke's report to her brother. She could even write it for him. But whenever she found herself between a rock and a hard place her choice would always be to stand and fight.

Tossing the phone on the bed, she grabbed her birthday shawl—which she'd slept with all night. Wrapping it round her shoulders, she arranged it carefully over a mountainous expanse of unfettered breast, crimping it into folds over her already Luke-eager nipples. Clutching her chest, as if that would somehow hold her heart steady, she remained frozen in place for around two seconds, and then sprang into action with a frantic scramble to clear up the mess. Not that there *was* much mess, as she didn't have many possessions.

Seizing a hairband from the side, she arranged her wild black bed-hair in what she hoped was a sexy, messy up-do— then groaned when she caught sight of herself in the flyblown mirror. How would Luke like her early-morning look? Not a lot, she guessed, fumbling with a tube of toothpaste. There was no time to clean her teeth, but she could rub some on her gums.

A glance out of the window confirmed that Luke had arrived from Planet Fabulous, where no one rose late or looked anything other than their best. Snug-fitting jeans moulded his powerful legs and displayed those alarming contours, while his cowboy boots only added to the sense of a man who didn't give a damn what anyone thought, let alone cared about fashion. Although the red sweater beneath his heavy-duty jacket gave a surprisingly cuddly twist to a man who looked strong enough to crush a rock in his fist.

Chomping on her lips to make them pinker, she already knew that any preparation she might make was too little too late. Luke looked amazing—even better than last night.

Sweeping a hopeless jumble of empty take-out boxes, crisp packets, chocolate wrappers and soda cans from the table onto the floor, she heeled them under the seat, making it to the door with barely a second to spare.

'Luke,' she said, forcing the tin door open with a well-timed kick. She stood, arms crossed, barring his way.

'Are we going to move inside, or are we going to stand out here getting wet?' he said, glancing up as a particularly malevolent storm cloud emptied its payload on the impossibly wide sweep of his shoulders.

'I'm sorry. Come in.'

Luke took in everything as he mounted the steps.

'Welcome to my world,' she said, fingers tensely white as she clutched the shawl.

'I hope you're joking.'

'Why would I be?' she said defensively.

'Where do I begin?' Luke cast a critical glance around.

'Well, you can leave right now if all you're here for is to find fault.'

Luke only had to ease position slightly to assure her that he had no intention of going anywhere.

CHAPTER SEVEN

He loves me... He loves me not. He loves me... He loves me not. At least not in the way I need him to love me.

LUKE'S expression might be fierce and dark, but she was ready for him. Remembering his teasing kisses, she *so* wasn't up for brotherly concern.

'Why are you here?' She tried to keep her voice light, remembering her determination that, whatever happened, somehow they must remain friends.

'Can't I even visit you now?' Luke's black brows snapped together.

'That depends.'

'On what?' He looked angrier than she had ever seen him. 'Whether I shake my head and tell you how this really looks to me, or if I pussyfoot around and pat you on the back for doing so well for yourself, Lucia?'

'That's hardly fair—'

'Can I sit down?' he interrupted.

'I think you better had,' she agreed tensely.

Luke couldn't even stand straight in the van, the ceiling was so low. And his shoulders took up most of the width. He was one of the few men, apart from her brothers, who could make her feel small. Bringing the cover down, he avoided sitting on her sheets. She liked that—but not the way Luke was acting. It reminded her too much of her brothers when they were in we-must-bring-Lucia-back-into-line mode.

'I can't believe you're living here, Lucia,' Luke ground out, confirming her thoughts.

'And what's wrong with here?' she said tensely.

'I doubt it's even safe.'

'Of course it's safe.'

'Rubbish.'

'If that's all you've come to say—'

'Not nearly,' he snarled. 'If you're working for Margaret, why aren't you sleeping at the guest house?'

'Have you been there recently?'

'It can't be any worse than here. This caravan's freezing. It's damp and the roof is leaking.'

'The roof can be repaired.'

Luke flashed a fast penetrating glance. 'By you?'

'I'll find someone.'

'Make it fast. And you'll pay them how?' he fired back in quick succession. 'You'd better ask your miracle workers to remove the spiders while they're at it,' he added, brandishing a really leggy one.

'Don't kill it.'

'What do you take me for?'

'You really don't want to know.' She watched transfixed as Luke transported the spider to the door, as if it were a priceless Fabergé egg he was holding in his large fist.

'You can't stay here,' he said, having deposited their hairy friend outside.

'Says who? You?'

'I won't let you,' Luke confirmed, resting one giant fist on his hip.

She knew that pose. It was like a big cat, kidding you it was relaxing just before it pounced. 'You can't stop me living here.' Tilting her chin, she directed a warning stare into Luke's eyes.

'Let me put this another way, Lucia. You don't have to stay here.'

'You're offering to pay for me to move somewhere better?' she guessed, trying to remember that determination to remain calm.

Luke shrugged.

'I've already told you—I don't need your help, Luke.'

'You clearly do,' he argued.

'Margaret needs me here on site.'

'If Margaret needs you why don't you clear a room at the guest house and move in?'

'I'm working on that as fast as I can.'

'Work faster.'

Luke's amber eyes had turned obsidian black, and they were very close—within touching distance. It would only take a step, a breath, one move by either of them... Luke's heat licked around her like a possession spell, or maybe a lust spell, showing him to be unashamedly male. It was far too much man for her damaged soul to handle.

She breathed a sigh of relief when Luke turned away to stare out of the window. Luke was her friend and she wanted it to stay that way. He had always been the one person she could confide in when her brothers ganged up on her. She wished she could confide in him now, one last time, and have Luke draw her into the safety of his embrace. But if he did that she wouldn't know when to stop, and then she would find herself in the ambit of Luke's world, rather than her own.

'The guest house is barely habitable,' she explained, drawing her business persona round her like a protective cloak.

'And sorting it out will be a long job,' Luke agreed turning round to face her.

'Are you about to make a move on the guest house?'

'Do *you* have some prior hold on it?' he said, watching her closely.

'So you *are* thinking of investing?'

'Margaret has expressed an interest and I have money to invest.'

If Luke and his stormtroopers moved in how real would her independence be then? As if she didn't know. 'It doesn't always come down to money, Luke.'

'Try doing anything without it, Lucia,' he flashed impatiently. 'Good intentions don't mend buildings. How are *you* going to set the guest house back on its feet?'

'By working every spare hour I've got. I've had a lot of extra shifts at the club recently.'

'I don't question your work ethic. I don't question your ability to turn things round, either, if funds are available—and I'd make sure they were. I've seen the work you've done on the *estancia*, and on the guest quarters at the family house on Isla del Fuego.'

'Desperation drove me to do that,' Lucia admitted, lightening up as she thought back. 'My brothers would be quite happy for their guests to live like horses in a barn if I didn't handle the décor and the organisation of the hospitality side of things for them.'

'Exactly,' Luke agreed. 'So I don't understand why the possibility of us working together here in Cornwall has never occurred to you.'

She couldn't have been more shocked. 'What are you suggesting?'

'Come and work for me,' Luke explained. 'I'd trust you to look after my best interests if I'm not around.'

Oh, great. Work for Luke, but without him being around. She would be just one more employee amongst the hundreds working for Forster, Inc.

She should be grateful for the opportunity, Lucia reminded herself. So how come she wasn't?

Because she wanted to paddle her own canoe, maybe?

'I've always been able to trust you, Lucia,' Luke continued, picking up on her change of heart. 'Nothing's changed where's that's concerned, has it?'

'Of course not.' She blanked London from her mind.

'Well?' he pressed.

'I'll think about it. But not if it means putting an official seal on you ordering me about.'

Luke laughed at that. 'Just don't take too long coming to a decision. I've got the money and resources waiting and ready to go. You've got the training and the flair. We both care about the guest house. It makes sense that you should work for me.'

'I could work *with* you, maybe,' she finessed.

'It's my investment on the line,' Luke stated firmly.

And Margaret's future. This wasn't about her pride, Lucia concluded. So could she work for Luke? The thought grated, but if she had an official role she could maybe dilute the Luke effect if he tried to wade in and take over. Didn't she owe that much to an old lady with no one else on her side?

'What's this?'

While she'd been thinking Luke had been making himself at home, and now he was staring at his centrefold, stuck to the wall with chewing gum. Why on earth hadn't she thought to pull the damn thing down before opening the door to him?

'That's my new dartboard,' she said lightly. 'Do you like it?'

'I didn't know you cared.'

'I don't.'

'You always were a terrible liar, Lucia.'

As Luke stared at her, she improvised, 'The girl who had the van before me must have stuck it up. I expect she used it to cover a crack.'

'Must have been a bloody big crack,' Luke murmured.

'Massive, I'm sure,' she mocked. 'I must admit I was surprised when I first saw it. I never took you for an attention-seeker, Luke.'

'Maybe because I'm not.'

'So…?'

'So your sister-in-law Holly persuaded me to let her run a magazine article to raise money for one of her charities. Holly just forgot to tell me when the photographers were coming.'

'Forgot on purpose, knowing Holly,' Lucia guessed, biting down on a smile. Holly could be ruthless when it came to landing a scoop. 'So the photographers caught you out?'

'No need to sound quite so pleased about it.'

Luke had brought his stubble-shaded face so close she could feel his heat warming her. 'You might have smiled for the camera,' she said, swinging away.

'They seemed satisfied with the shots they took, so I guess angry men sell more magazines than smiling men.'

'Well, I don't like angry men.'

'Don't you?'

'Don't act so surprised, Luke. You know I don't. I've always preferred mild-mannered men who are kind and thoughtful.'

'And who have just stepped off the cover of a book of fairy-tales? Get real, Lucia.' Luke's voice turned hard. 'Or are you going to live in that fantasy world of yours for ever?'

'My world seems pretty real to me right now.' And she knew more about the real world than she cared to, which was something Luke definitely didn't need to know.

'Does this real world of yours turn on daydreams or actions?' he demanded. 'I hope for Margaret's sake you've thought this through. And as for those hard, driven men? You're a hopeless liar, Lucia. You *love* hard, driven men. You should do. You've grown up with four of them. You just think it's fashionable to pretend that you don't.'

'Why on earth would I do that?' she flashed as the temperature soared between them.

'Hell if I know,' Luke fired back with an angry gesture.

'Since when has what I feel become your business?'

'You're right,' he said, turning for the door. 'I have absolutely no interest in you whatsoever.'

'Where are you going?' She realised as Luke swung around to stare at her that the desperation in her voice had pealed out like a klaxon.

'I'm going to check this cooker. You can't use it,' Luke added, having given the sagging heap of tin a cursory examination. 'And it can't be repaired, so don't even think of exercising your new-found practical skills.'

'Why would I be practical when you and my brothers have snatched things out of my hands for as long as I can remember?'

'Only so you couldn't beat us over the head with them.'

True. 'So why are you here, Luke? To offer me a job, or to compile a list of my failings for Nacho?'

'I'm not sure I want such a difficult employee.'

'Too much for you?' she taunted, mellowing a little.

'As it happens, I didn't come here to offer you a job. I came to tie up some loose ends with Margaret, so everything we've been talking about may have to be put on hold.'

Until Margaret had given her agreement to Luke buying into the business, Lucia surmised, knowing she mustn't do anything to spoil Margaret's chances. Maybe co-operation was the key—just so long as it was co-operation and not annihilation.

'Do you ever think back to those holidays, Lucia?'

Whoa, cowboy! That was a nifty change of tack. But Luke had always known how to reach in for her heart and squeeze it tight. And there was nothing like poignant memories that joined them both to do that. 'I think about those holidays all the time,' she said honestly. And then, because she didn't want Luke knowing how that made her feel, she added waspishly, 'You always were such a charmer.'

'You haven't changed much yourself,' Luke countered.

But she had changed. *So much.*

He was lying, thought Luke. Lucia had changed beyond all recognition. Yes, she was all grown up, but there were shadows behind her eyes that had never used to be there, and they worried him. Surely she couldn't still be upset after the confrontation with that drunk last night?

'You're over last night's drama, aren't you?' he checked. 'The drunk?' he expanded when she frowned.

'Of course I'm over it.'

But her cheeks flushed red when he held her gaze. So was she remembering when he'd kissed her? *He* was. 'Let's get back to your reasons for coming down to Cornwall,' he said, seeking safer ground.

'What about it?'

'Is there anything else you'd like to share?'

'You never give up, do you?' she said, laughing as if he was making too much of things.

Her laughter sounded hollow to him. 'No, I don't,' he confirmed.

'You always were so suspicious, Luke.'

You bet he was. 'Of course I'm curious to know why you left London, why you came back here. And why you've decided to stay.'

'That's three questions.'

She laughed again, but it still rang false.

'Confiding in a friend isn't a sign of weakness, Lucia.'

'I don't feel the need to confide in anyone, Luke. And I certainly don't need you as my shrink.'

'That is good news,' he agreed.

'Why?' she said.

'Because I'd need a sixth sense and a doctorate in divination before I could sort you out.' But as his stare dropped to the curve of her lips he wondered if it really would be all that hard to sort Lucia out.

CHAPTER EIGHT

My to-do list has collapsed. I have hardly ticked off any items, and even those I have tried to tick off I've bodged. What I really need is a relationship counsellor. Luke has stirred memories I have always tried to skirt around, making me look at some of the least comfortable of them head-on. He has made me realise that I wrote my to-do list at a time when all I could think was: If I had my time, this is what I would do with it.

I wrote that list so confidently at age fourteen, hardly realising how much more complicated life could be than a series of goals to enhance my physical appearance. What about my heart? What about a to-do list for my heart?

'WOULD you like something to drink?' she asked the warrior currently taking up every available inch of space in her caravan whilst throwing his weight around like all her brothers combined. It was the least she could do, she convinced herself. After all, Luke had offered her a job that might even have a wage attached. And he'd given the caravan a health-check—not that that had worked out so well.

'That would be good,' he confirmed. 'Just don't give me one of those glasses on the shelf over the cooker, with a coating of dust and a dead fly garnish.'

She laughed. She hadn't even noticed there were glasses on that shelf. Back to the drawing board where cleaning was concerned, Lucia concluded, and with a head full of scouring powder and dishcloths this time, instead of Luke. 'How about a can of soda?'

'Whatever you've got, sweetheart.'

'I'm not your sweetheart.' She stalled, realising she'd given too much away by snapping like that. How often had she dreamed of Luke murmuring endearments, knowing he never would? A quick glance was enough to reassure her that Luke hadn't even registered the sting in her words.

This was like trying to contain a tiger in a very small box, Lucia concluded as Luke performed the seemingly impossible feat of squeezing his powerful body into the smallest of spaces between the bunk-cum-bench and a chipped Formica table.

'What happened to this place?' he murmured, staring out of the window.

'I guess the world grew tired of St Oswalds and moved on.'

'I can't see anyone studying their reflection in a rock pool,' Luke agreed, his sweeping ebony brows lifting with amusement as he glanced at her.

'I wasn't looking at myself. I was studying wildlife, if you must know.'

'I was pretty wild back in those days,' he commented dryly.

'You are *so* full of it. I wasn't looking at *you*,' she insisted heatedly, knowing full well that the whole point of sitting sentry by that rock pool had been to make sure she was in position when Luke came thundering by.

He'd always chosen the wildest pony in the bunch so he could thrash her brothers, but when Luke had returned to the guest house he'd been all gloss and manners. An only child, idolised by his parents, Luke had never let them down. When Luke came down to dinner his necktie would be perfectly knotted, his hair neat and his shoes highly polished. Leave him with her brothers for half an hour and Luke turned feral.

It had been a kickback against his strict upbringing, she realised now, remembering how unbelievably sexy she had found the transformation from strait-laced Luke to an impossibly wild version. And now he was somewhere in between. Formidably successful in business, Luke was a barbarian, unstoppable and unbelievably sexy, on the polo field. What he was like in private she had no idea—not really.

'Those were great days,' he said thoughtfully, shifting position in a way that suggested Luke's temporarily confined body was cramped like a coiled spring.

'Yes, they were,' she agreed, trying to forget the glances that had passed between them when they were teenagers.

She'd had to be so careful not to let her brothers see how she felt about Luke. Everything about the invisible bond between them had been breath-stealing and forbidden. And had quite possibly only existed in her imagination, Lucia conceded silently, since normally Luke had barely acknowledged her existence when her brothers were around.

Her brothers weren't here now...

It made no difference. She wasn't about to throw herself at Luke and make a bigger fool of herself than she already had by flirting and then flinching when the fear came roaring back.

'Those holidays were the highlight of my year,' he admitted, shaking her out of the reverie.

'You being an only child, I guess down-time with my brothers was quite a novelty.'

'That's one way of putting it,' Luke agreed, his lips tugging as he thought back.

She picked up his empty can just for the excuse to turn away and put it in the trash. Even then she could feel the heat of his stare on her back. Just what exactly was Luke thinking?

'That's the connection between us,' he said, making her swing round.

'What is?' she demanded.

'You were the only girl in a family with four hell-raising brothers, and I was an only child in a family with ramrods up its spine. Both of us were outsiders, Lucia. We just didn't see it that way back then.'

'So fill in the gaps, Luke. What have you been doing since I last saw you?'

'Making money. Building companies. Making sure my father can retire with honour. Nursing the family's charitable foundation back to health. What about you, Lucia?'

'You first,' she said stubbornly. 'Why did you come back here?'

Luke cocked his head as he stared away from her. 'Same reason as you, I expect. I've been trying to recapture something I've lost.'

'Freedom,' she said, thinking out loud.

'I'm free enough,' Luke argued, 'but I do miss the good times we used to have here. When you can choose to holiday anywhere in the world it's surprising how you hanker after the familiar. Only St Oswalds wasn't the way I remembered it when I came back.'

'No, it's falling apart,' she agreed.

'So I'll do something about it,' he said with a shrug.

'And so will I,' she said, staking her claim.

'What are your plans, Lucia?'

She felt defensive suddenly. How feeble they would sound compared to his. Her plans included working as hard as she could and trying to get the villagers to help too. She wasn't ready to admit that her plans also included the rebuilding of Lucia Acosta, brick by unsmothered brick—preferably without hang-ups this time. But she had to admit there were possibilities to them working together. Luke was a highly successful businessman, while she understood the hospitality industry and how to make guests happy.

'Were you planning to invest your own money, or are your brothers backing you?' Luke pressed as the silence ticked by.

'I'm sure Nacho must have told you that he pays me an allowance like a trust fund brat?'

'He didn't, actually. I think Nacho cares a lot more about you than you give him credit for, Lucia.'

And now she felt guilty. 'I know he does,' she admitted quietly. 'If you must know, I divert the money Nacho gives me into a charity.'

Luke shrugged. 'You don't have to explain yourself to me, Lucia.'

But she wanted to. 'Standing on my own two feet doesn't mean I don't appreciate or love my brothers any less. I just don't want handouts from anyone, Luke—and that includes you.'

'If Margaret agrees to me buying in I'll make you earn your money.'

'Then we might have a deal.'

'Let's thrash a few things through first,' he said, standing to tug off his jacket.

'You're far too big for a caravan,' she observed as Luke ducked his head.

'And you're far too spoiled,' Luke countered. 'There's plenty of room in here for both of us.'

If they were welded together, Luke might be right. 'You think?'

'I know. You just have to be well organised, Lucia.'

'I'm trying,' she said.

'You certainly are,' he agreed. 'Why don't you sit down?' Luke patted the bed by his side.

Because there was nowhere to sit without sitting on top of

him. She settled for perching awkwardly on the very edge of the bed, but even then their thighs were touching.

Luke rested his chin on his shoulder to stare at her. 'Well, this is cosy—but there are plenty of better places I can think of to chat through your terms and conditions.'

'Like the Grand?' she cut in.

Luke's lips pressed down. He'd been sure she would fold and agree to let him book a room for her.

'Let's get one thing straight, Luke. If I work for you, I stand on my own two feet. I don't commute from the Grand. I live here—on site.'

'I won't let you stay here.'

'You can't stop me.'

'Nostalgia is a powerful force, Lucia, as I would be the first to admit, but you should never allow it to cloud your judgement. You can work here and live down the road.'

'And travel in by town car? No way, Luke. I've left that life behind, and now I'm going to live my life my way.'

Raking his hair, he somehow managed to keep his mouth shut until they had both calmed down. He had vowed not to get involved. 'Let me give you some facts, Lucia. The guest house is so far gone this project might not even work with my money backing it. The Sundowner was my first choice when I decided I wanted to reinstate Polo on the Beach, but when I made enquiries I was told the guest house had been failing for years—'

'Who told you this?' she interrupted.

'My second choice: the Grand.'

'So the small local guest house finds itself in difficulties and the nearby behemoth does its best to stamp it out of business?' She shook her head. 'I can't believe you went along with that, Luke. It's not what I'd call neighbourly.'

'If you're serious about working in the hotel industry it's

time you learned how to get on with the competition. Keep your friends close and your enemies closer, Lucia.'

'Says the oracle?'

'It's a basic rule of business.'

'Well, thanks for the advice, Luke. I guess I'll just have to make my own mistakes.'

'And if you're thinking about sleeping another night under this roof,' he said, giving it a blow with his fist that set the whole place shaking, 'I'd advise you not to. It's freezing outside and you don't have any heating. There isn't even a lock on the door.'

'Margaret has lived alone at the guest house for most of her life.'

'Because Margaret *has* to,' Luke pointed out. 'You don't have to. You didn't have to live in at the hotel in London. You could have stayed at the family penthouse.'

In spite of her best efforts the temperature was rising. 'In the best part of town?'

'It would have been a roof over your head. Just as taking a room at the Grand wouldn't kill you.'

'And how is living at the family penthouse or running up your bill at the Grand supposed to make me independent, Luke? I'm safe here. The fact that Margaret has lived alone for all these years should tell you something.'

'It does,' Luke agreed. 'It tells me Margaret has no option, because she has nowhere else to go. It tells me the Sundowner isn't just failing—it has already failed. And what are you going to do about it? You don't have any money. You've given it all away.'

'Says one of the biggest charity supporters in the world.'

'I can afford to give. You can't. You've got no practical skills.'

'I learned a lot on my degree course,' she argued.

'Like what?' he scoffed. 'Fifty ways to fold a napkin?'

'That's *it*!' Lucia exploded, completely forgetting the disparity in their size as she sprang up.

Luke stood too. 'Before I go anywhere you're going to hear some home truths, and you won't like them, Lucia. You're great at starting things, but you've never finished anything in your life.'

'Get out!' She was beyond anger now. 'I should have known better than to think you are any different to my brothers. Go on!' she yelled with a furious gesture, pummelling impotent fists against Luke's stone chest. 'Get out of my caravan.'

'I'm not going anywhere without you.' He planted himself in her way.

'So what are you going to do? Throw me over your shoulder and carry me out?'

'If I have to.'

They glared at each other. Passion had never run higher between them, but she wasn't prepared for what happened next—not nearly. Yanking her close, Luke kissed her, and his firm, sexy lips worked their magic.

Of course she fought him. Of course she tried to push him away. But Luke was a rock—a fierce, ravenous, hot rock. Her nipples tightened and heat pooled between her thighs. She'd thought she'd never be able to feel this way again, but her reaction to Luke was like the plug of a volcano blowing after centuries of hot lava building up. She had to hold her hand across her mouth when he abruptly let her go, as if that could hide the proof of her arousal. She was shaking—and not from fear. Luke hadn't given fear time to set in. She was shaking with shock, with anger and with desire.

'You're vulnerable,' Luke said flatly.

'And you were just proving your point?' she demanded incredulously. Her brain cells clinked feverishly into line. That hadn't been a brush, a tease or even a trial kiss. That had been a full-on, body-melting, fear-destroying sensual assault that could never, ever be mistaken for a brotherly peck.

'I'm just putting you back in touch with reality,' Luke said, managing to look sexier than ever as he leaned back against the door.

'Nice technique you have for doing that. Am I supposed to thank you?' It was hard to do battle with her very insistent pulse throbbing, but she drove on. 'I think you should go now.'

'I'm not going anywhere until you calm down.'

'Please yourself.'

Her chest was heaving with...yes, passion. But as they glared at each other she thought of her own climb back, her fight to regain her old self, and Margaret's dream to restore her guest house. Plus, wasn't Luke's offer of a job the perfect opportunity to take that first step on her own emotional to-do list?

'Maybe I have found it hard to finish what I've started in the past,' she admitted stiffly, 'but I'm totally committed to what has to be done here. It means a lot to me.'

'As it does to me,' Luke said quietly, his stare dropping to her lips.

'Okay,' she said, coming to a decision. 'I'll make a deal with you. When I've proved myself, maybe—just maybe, mark you—I'll kiss you back.'

Luke laughed, and the tension between them started to ease, but they both knew that any thought of them being like brother and sister in future was out of the window. Lucia only wished she could tell Luke that she would *never* be able to make good on all the sexual tension between them, but how could she admit that she was damaged and tainted and frightened? Or that she could handle a business relationship, but anything else between them was impossible?

'At least life won't be dull from now on,' he remarked,

eyeing her with humour. 'Though whether it will match up to your experience in London…'

She flinched. Damn it, she actually flinched—and Luke saw it. She hadn't seen that one coming. She should have known Luke would never let it go until she told him the truth about the day that sleazy concierge had decided a pampered Argentinian princess would be easy pickings. Just thinking about it now made her feel sick.

'Lucia?'

She must have paled. 'What?' she said, swallowing back bile.

'Why won't you tell me what happened in London?'

'You still don't get it, do you, Luke? I can handle it.'

He held his hands up palms flat in apparent surrender, and in fairness to Luke she had relied on him and her brothers for so long it was no wonder he felt the need to ride in and save her like the White Knight. But she had changed, and things would be different from now on. She needed no one to save her.

'When you speak to Nacho, just tell him you've seen me and I'm safe. You can also tell him that I've got a roof over my head.'

'A leaking tin roof.'

'And that I won't do anything stupid,' she added firmly.

Unfortunately these were famous last words. As she moved towards the door she somehow managed to spill the contents of the birthday gift bag from her friends, and as Luke stared down in dumb amazement, he saw laid out in front of him, like some offering to a *yoni* god, an industrial-sized packet of condoms, a pair of red crotchless knickers and a very adult toy.

'Nothing stupid?' he murmured.

'Goodbye, Luke.' She had no intention of explaining her gifts to him. Where the job was concerned Luke could call her to account, but the gifts from her friends were none of his damn business.

'Let me know if you're going to take the job, Lucia.'

'I think you know I will.'

'Then as soon as I have an agreement from Margaret I'll have a contract drawn up for you,' he said, giving her a keen glance before opening the door.

She closed her eyes as Luke left the van, but she could still feel him in every fibre of her being. Being with Luke was like brushing the edge of a storm she longed to be swept up in. But if she allowed that to happen everything would be out of her control and under Luke's dominion. She could work for him. She would just have to keep her feelings in check. She *must*. She couldn't bear for Luke to know the humiliating truth.

CHAPTER NINE

I'm not doing so well when it comes to ticking goals off my list—but that's only because I'm impatient and try to take things too fast. And I have my heart set on one man.

So, what have I learned?

I'm frightened of sex.

I'm frightened of Luke finding out I'm frightened of sex and why...

Were I not frightened of sex there would still be a problem, because sex with Luke Forster is never going to happen. I'm obviously not his type—maybe I'm not good enough for him. Luke has sampled several kisses and shows minimal enthusiasm at the prospect of sampling more. Fair enough. If he tried more than kisses I'd probably run a mile.

So it's back to the start of my list with an open mind. If I remain focused I should reach number ten in no time. And if number ten doesn't involve sex with Luke, that's no big deal. The way I feel about sex right now, I'd sooner have an ice cream.

The new plan:

Concentrate on practical matters and forget about my heart. Unlike the path of Cupid's arrow, practical can be planned out in bullet points.

• I have a job at the guest house.

- *The guest house has nine bedrooms.*
- *Sort out the smallest of them for live-in staff.*
- *Live-in staff—that's me! My new quarters will be fabulous when they're finished. 'When', being the operative word.*

TAKING the engine to its limits, he aimed a blow at the steering wheel. Nothing helped ease the frustration inside him.

'Thanks, Nacho,' he murmured, adding a few more choice curses.

If he hadn't gone looking for Lucia he wouldn't have found her—wouldn't want her as he did. He wouldn't have danced with her, touched her. He wouldn't have the mystery of her time in London driving him insane right now.

There was only one way forward. Once he was sure she was physically safe, he was going to retrace Lucia's tiny footsteps inch by scrupulous inch until he found out what she wasn't telling him.

The attraction between them had been on the back boiler for years. It had simmered at the wedding and boiled over in the caravan. His primal instinct told him to carry her off. Not to listen to any excuses. He could just imagine Lucia's response if he tried *that* approach.

Might be fun...

Lucia gave a happy sigh. For a girl who had grown up slaving over brothers as soon as she could hold a mop, there was nothing more satisfying than cleaning up after herself. The caravan might still be shabby, but at least there were no more dusty glasses lurking on forgotten shelves. It even smelled fantastic. She kept telling herself that cleaning would help channel the energy left over from Luke's visit. It hadn't even scraped the surface.

Flopping down on the bench, she glanced at his poster. She

grabbed a magazine. Now it was just a case of finding a page that wasn't devoted to 'Different Sex Positions for Every Day of the Month…' 'Sex Positions for Your Sign of the Zodiac…' 'Hot Sex in Surprising Places…' 'Is that all anyone thinks about?' she demanded, glaring at Luke's centrefold.

Probably, Lucia concluded, thanks to posters like Luke's. Flinging the magazine aside, she leaned back against the bench, trying not to think about sex or her hang-ups. And then she leapt up again, colliding with the shelf.

'What the…?' She jumped around, nursing her head. 'Luke?' Her heart roared into action as a vehicle door banged.

Was Luke back?

What could that mean?

She knelt on the bench to stare out. Her excitement evaporated. It wasn't Luke with his sexy, brooding look, let alone Luke bearing armfuls of flowers with an adoring expression on his swarthy, disreputable face. It was Luke in practical mode, climbing out of a humungous pick-up truck. There was a hook on the back of the truck which he was now attaching to a fixing on the front of the caravan.

He might have warned her! Bracing her hands against the walls as the van rocked up and down, she finally made it to the door. She had to bounce off it a couple of times before she could force it open, by which time she was stoked.

'What the *hell* are you doing?'

'You might want to wait in the truck while I do this,' Luke suggested, without bothering to glance up.

'I'm not going anywhere until you tell me what you're doing.'

Luke's tousled head lifted and his fierce gold stare pierced hers. 'What does it look like, Lucia?'

'You're hitching up the caravan. And taking it where?' she demanded. 'If this is just another ruse to get me to move out—'

Luke straightened up to his full ridiculous height. 'There's no subterfuge involved in what I'm doing. I'm going to tow the caravan a safe distance away from the cliff.' His eyes narrowed. 'You *must* have felt the wind lifting it?'

The cliff did seem dangerously close, now she came to look. 'I have felt it rattling sometimes,' she admitted, distracted by how thick Luke's nut-brown hair was as the wind tossed it about, making it catch on his sharp black stubble.

'And the jacks are broken so the caravan is resting on three wheels.'

That did not sound good. 'Okay, thank you.'

'Go and get something on before you freeze to death. You're soaked through. Your clothes are sticking to your body.'

They were?

And her nipples were nicely puckered too.

'I'll pack the breakables,' she called back, retreating into the caravan.

'Here!' Luke called her back. 'Before you come outside again put this on.'

He reached out to hand her his jacket, but before she could take hold of it he draped it round her shoulders.

'Now, let me go and hitch this thing up,' he said brusquely, turning away.

Wind and rain apparently made no impact on Luke's mighty jean-clad frame. She leaned her head against the doorframe for a moment, watching him, waiting until he had disappeared round the side of the caravan. His clothes were nicely moulded to his body, and as she pulled his jacket close she could only be happy when she found that it was still Luke-warm.

She packed up quickly and then went to wait in the pick-up. Resting her head against the worn leather seat, she listened to Luke's music tracks as she absorbed the scent of truck oil, spice and soap. The warmth in the cab, with its overlay of Luke, made her feel all homey and contented. Her imagination soon took flight.

And quickly came down to earth again when Luke joined her in the cab with a blast of cold air and a blaze of energy, following it up by barely acknowledging her before starting the engine. She was taking a chunk out of his day. That was obvious. Luke kissing her was a long-ago fantasy. He'd tried it and parked it.

Releasing the brake, he inched the truck forward. The sound of creaking and grinding was alarming as the old caravan moved reluctantly off its site.

'Hang on!' Luke exclaimed as they hit a pothole.

She gasped as the truck lurched and she fell into him.

Shrugging her off, Luke turned to glance over his shoulder. 'Lucky escape.'

He was probably right, Lucia thought, moving as far away as possible.

'This is the place,' he said, when they reached the shelter of some trees. 'I scouted round earlier. The caravan will be private here, and it's safe on level ground.'

Which was more than *she* was, Lucia reflected ruefully. 'Do you want me to get out and check round?'

'You stay there,' he said, springing down.

The caravan was soon unhitched, and when Luke climbed back into the cab he looked at her. 'Okay, you can go now,' he prompted, gesturing with his chin towards the door.

'Where are you going?'

'To the Grand for a shower,' Luke offered, his brooding amber gaze alive with the first humour of the day. 'Is that a problem for you?'

'No,' she said, as if she couldn't care less. She had thought he might stay...

'My jacket?' Luke prompted as she reached for the door.

If she was waiting for another kiss that experiment was clearly over, she concluded, tugging it off and handing it over.

'Let this be an end to the risk-taking,' Luke advised.

So don't come round again, she thought, staring him in the eyes. But when her gaze dropped to his lips she was prompted to promise fervently, 'No more risks of any kind.'

Slapping the side of the truck as she got out, she walked back to the caravan. She felt hollow as she watched Luke drive away. She shouldn't have kissed him. She shouldn't have flirted with him. She shouldn't have allowed herself to think for one moment that they could be anything but friends. Maybe she'd spoiled even that. Maybe Luke's offer of a job was just a way of keeping her in one place so her brothers always knew where she was.

Did she have so little confidence?

Where Luke was concerned? Yes. It was hard to feel upbeat when she felt as if she'd lost him—when she felt as if the Luke she'd used to know didn't exist any more. And she missed that man.

Lucia's heat remained in his jacket all the way back to the hotel. He tried to ignore how that made him feel, and settled into accepting some facts that couldn't be changed. Lucia was his best friend's sister. She was the closest thing he had to a sister. But he wanted her.

And Nacho?

He would tell Nacho the truth—that there was no quick fix for a woman of Lucia's temperament, and that her brother would just have to be patient for once.

And how patient was Luke?

Some things never changed, Luke reflected as he glanced into the rearview mirror, as if he might catch one last glimpse of Lucia. He would always care about her.

He smiled as he wondered how long it would be before the parcels arrived, and if she would send them straight back.

* * *

She was about to leave for the guest house when there was a knock on the door. Throwing her weight against it, she stood staring in blank surprise at the man in uniform standing outside a big green van.

'Delivery for Ms Acosta?' the man said, checking the label on one of the packages he was holding.

'That's me,' Lucia confirmed, 'but I haven't ordered anything.'

'Then it must be a gift,' the delivery man said, sticking a clipboard beneath her nose. 'Sign here, please.'

There was only one person in the world who would order a hamper from London's most famous luxury goods store. There was only one person who knew her address in Cornwall.

As soon as she had loaded everything inside, she picked up her phone and called Luke. 'What do you think you're doing?' she demanded the moment he picked up. 'Why are you sending me food parcels? I'm not that desperate.'

'I can't send a few treats for you and Margaret to share?'

'We don't need charity.'

'My PA handles returns—speak to her.'

She sat back, stung.

'Goodbye, Lucia. Enjoy the bacon and eggs.'

She stared at the dead phone in dismay. This Luke was far removed from the Luke she had provoked, teased and taunted when they were younger; she didn't even know him.

Hadn't she changed too?

And it wasn't just a hamper of food. There was everything anyone might need if they were starting out on their own for the first time—good towels, sheets, throws, decent pillows.

'This will all have to go back,' she told Luke's poster. But as his arrogant face sent a scorching challenge back and she lifted one of the pillows and held it to her face she wondered if she wasn't being just a little hasty.

And ungrateful, Lucia conceded. She tried to call Luke

again, to thank him. She wanted to tell him he should take the money out of her wages. But he wasn't picking up.

He didn't take her call until later that day, and she was rather put off her stride to hear Luke's husky tone backed by a soundtrack of languidly swishing water. Trying to blank the X-rated mental images that evoked, she said hello.

'Hey,' Luke murmured lazily, 'this is a nice surprise.'

That Luke hadn't declined her call? It certainly was. He sounded unimaginably pleased, as if something big had gone down. But far worse was listening to him groaning with pleasure as he eased his position in the bath.

'My assistant did okay for you?' he prompted. 'Do you like the stuff she chose?'

Another disturbing mental image flashed into her mind. This one involved an extravagantly beautiful PA—something like the Technicolor blonde—discussing her with Luke before rushing off to carry out his mercy mission.

'Mary said it was no trouble to pick out some essentials for you while she was shopping for her grandchildren's Christmas presents, so I hope she got it right?'

Lucia's shoulders slumped. She felt such an idiot. 'Please tell Mary I'm very grateful. And thank you, Luke. Just don't do it again.'

'Do what again?' he murmured, in a voice that spoke of warm soapy water and tropical ambient heat. 'Buy you gifts?'

She stroked the shawl. 'I don't need handouts.'

Luke's laugh was a rumble deep in his chest. 'I was just being neighbourly, Lucia. I thought you approved of that?'

There was more swishing water, until all she could see was Luke's massive body, wet, tanned and gleaming, his hard muscles flexing—along with a whole raft of other X-rated images.

'Just so long as you're not trying to buy me off.'

'Can I do that with a few rashers of bacon and half a dozen eggs?'

She smiled as she hugged the phone. 'You'd be relieved to be rid of me.'

'I certainly would,' he agreed.

'I have every intention of paying you back.'

'I would expect nothing less,' he murmured, sighing contentedly. She imagined him sinking lower in the bath as he demanded drowsily, 'Is that it?'

'Am I keeping you?'

'Yes. What are you doing for the rest of the day?'

Trying not to think about you buck-naked in a warm, soapy bath. 'There isn't much left of today, but I have cleared a bedroom at the guest house, so at some point I'll be decorating and sorting it out. I don't have time to chat.'

'Maybe I'll drop by later to see how you're getting on.'

'There's no need,' she said as her heart rate went off the scale.

'I'll bring some decent coffee with me.'

'We've got good coffee.'

'Excellent. Start grinding. I could murder a cup.'

'Call room service.'

Luke laughed as he cut the line.

Thoroughly shaken, she threw herself back against the cold tin wall in an attempt to steady her breathing and consider the facts. If Luke did come round, as he had threatened, Margaret would be pleased. And this was all about work now. Luke never backed off once he'd got the bit between his teeth, and while she didn't have Luke's money or influence, her background and training—honed by four demanding brothers—meant she could bring quite a lot to the party too.

Work with Luke?

Work she could do. And she couldn't deny that the prospect of butting heads with him on a regular basis held massive appeal.

CHAPTER TEN

There is a lot to be said for home-cooking.

East, west, home's best?

It certainly is. Try looking at what's been under your nose for years.

No! Not the moustache-in-need-of-a-wax, stupid! Luke.

MARGARET had been baking up a storm. There was a non-stop supply of succulent sausage and crispy bacon for all the people who had turned up to work. Luke had announced his intention to fast-track the project, which was great news for everyone—apart from Lucia, who wondered if she was the only one to receive the news with mixed feelings. Luke was experienced in business, while this was her first big project, and Luke wasn't exactly noted for his tolerance levels. If she didn't make the grade she'd be out on her ear.

There were more important things than her pride, Lucia concluded as she took a spoonful of Margaret's soup. 'Your cooking is what St Oswalds has been missing.'

'Do you really think so?' Margaret smiled happily as she turned back to the cooker. 'If you stopped working at that club—stopped being Anita and started being the girl I used to know—all this would be worthwhile for me. You *have* given your notice in?'

'Yes, I have,' Lucia confirmed.

The two women had become close, and Lucia had never been anything but open with Margaret about the reason for her name-change. All sorts of busybodies frequented the club, and though Lucia had never made a magazine spread in her life, and doubted anyone knew her face, the name Acosta might have raised suspicions, since the family had spent many of their summers in the area.

'I'm so glad you're going to be working with Luke.'

Lucia's chin shot up. There was a distinct difference between working *for* and working *with*. She knew Luke would think so.

'I don't understand business, which is how I got myself into this mess in the first place,' Margaret was busy explaining, 'so I'd like *you* to be my caretaker-manager.'

'Manage the Sundowner?' Lucia exclaimed. 'Have you spoken to Luke about this?' She could already hear the thunderclaps approaching.

Margaret shrugged. 'I still have some say. You'll balance Luke out. You both believe in the Sundowner, and while you have the training and flair Luke can handle the financial side of things. In my eyes it's the perfect partnership. I want you front of house, Lucia.'

'Only until you feel ready to take over,' Lucia said firmly. 'Thank you,' she added quietly. 'I can't tell you what it means to have your confidence.'

'If you ask me, Lucia, people should have been placing their confidence in you a long time ago.'

Lucia laughed. 'You've met my brothers. They don't think I can tie my own shoelaces yet. But I won't let you down.'

'I don't think for one moment you will, and as soon as Luke returns from London I'm going to tell him my decision.'

'Luke's in London?' Lucia heard nothing else.

'Some business he needed to look into, I think he said.'

Margaret shook her head. 'I really don't know,' she said vaguely. 'Why are you looking so worried, Lucia?'

'No reason.' But Lucia's mind had started flying in all directions.

'Why don't you go into town and spoil yourself for a change?' Margaret was suggesting. 'Buy yourself a couple of suits in anticipation of the guest house opening?'

'Go into town? Good idea,' Lucia agreed distractedly, pulling herself round.

Her life was changing so rapidly it was hard to keep up. But she had to—though she doubted she could relax, as Margaret had suggested, for wondering what Luke was doing in London. Some sixth sense told her that whatever it was it wasn't good.

As the tall, imposing individual emerged through the swing doors of the exclusive London hotel pedestrians shied away. Rather than step forward to ask if the man required a cab, the uniformed doorman stepped back.

Tugging off his heavy jacket, Luke tossed it into the back of the SUV, which he'd parked aggressively in a no-parking zone. Springing into the driver's seat, he placed a call to Lucia's brother in Argentina.

'The problem's sorted,' he confirmed without expression.

He had tracked down the man he now knew had attacked Lucia, and had resolved the situation to his personal satisfaction. Cracking his knuckles, he gunned the engine and swung the vehicle into the slow-moving London traffic. In a few hours' time he would be back in Cornwall, and Lucia would be none the wiser.

He reorganised his diary on the way back to Cornwall. He wouldn't be returning home right away, as originally planned. His business interests were well managed and could survive without him for a few more days. Whether she knew it or not, Lucia needed him—and that took precedence over everything.

He was going to stay on at the Grand until the guest house project was up and running and he was sure she was okay. Learning what he had in London had convinced him that what Lucia Acosta needed was a guardian angel.

Though after today a *dark* angel might be a more fitting description, Luke concluded as his senses roared at the thought of seeing her again. So he was going to see Lucia again. No big deal.

Try telling that to his libido.

After a quick shower at the Grand he checked out the stubble situation. He badly needed to shave, but he was impatient to see Lucia again. He threw on a pair of jeans and while he was buckling the belt he thought about her. He thought about Lucia all the time. So what if she brought mayhem to his life? There was never a dull moment when they were together. And the thought that someone had hurt her...

Breaking through to Lucia was his next and most important project. She couldn't shut out what had happened in London for ever. She mustn't be allowed to. It would damage her.

Ruffling his hair in a token nod to grooming, he grabbed the phone when it rang and smiled as he checked the number.

'Margaret.' He strained to hear Lucia's voice in the background, but he couldn't make out what she was saying. 'It's never too late to eat, Margaret. Thanks for the invitation.'

The shave could definitely wait.

She was working her socks off in an attempt to forget Margaret had invited Luke for supper. Luke having mysterious business in London was something she preferred not to think about, so she'd chosen displacement activity instead. Where practical matters were concerned she already knew her strength lay in design and layout, and then in sourcing the right people to do the job, but today it felt as if she had more to prove.

Today it felt as if she had everything to prove.

It was the concierge effect chipping away at her self-confidence, Lucia suspected. Just hearing Luke was in London had brought it all back to her. Fortunately fate had played into her hands. While she was rooting around in the attic she'd found a bolt of fabric and a staple gun. A stool was a good place to start—nice and simple. And just think of the money they could save if she could upholster some of the stuff herself instead of sending it out. How hard could it be? Stool. Stuffing. Cut a template for the fabric...

She found out how hard as Luke pulled into the yard. Her increasingly urgent calls to Margaret had met with zero response as she tried frantically to detach the sleeve of her uniform from the stool. Not that her heart wasn't playing Jai-alai at the thought of seeing Luke again, but...

Be careful what you wish for?

She had wanted to surprise Margaret with her frugal ways, but had not pictured accidentally stapling herself to the stool as a possible outcome. She could just imagine what Luke would say.

And...

Oh, good. He was peering through the window.

He had driven to the guest house the same way he rode a horse—flat out. He couldn't wait to get back to Cornwall and hold Lucia in his arms to reassure her that anyone who tried to hurt her again would have to get past him first. His pulse had surged when he'd seen her at the window as he drove up. He'd expected she would get up and open the door for him, but instead she was just staring at him. And if he hadn't known better he would have said that was alarm on her face. Even having raked his hair into some semblance of order, he reasoned he probably did look like a bandit.

'I'm not interrupting anything, am I?' he demanded, finding her alone in the room.

Luke looked so gloriously wolfish for a moment she couldn't speak. She had never seen him looking this pumped off a polo field. 'Welcome back,' she said carefully. Remaining seated, she turned at an awkward angle to hide the fact that there was a stool attached to her arm.

'What have you got there?' Luke said, coming closer to investigate.

'It's an antique,' she explained offhandedly, dragging in his warm, spicy scent, laced with a refreshing shot of bracing sea air.

'An antique?' Luke murmured, his lips pressing down attractively.

'Yes…' She met his assessing gaze with a challenging look, but she couldn't read if Luke had learned anything in London from a stare that was brooding and amused. 'I thought I'd restore the stool,' she explained, clinging to something safe and mundane.

'Do you mean you're re-covering it?' Luke glanced at the remains of the fabric strewn across the floor.

She was the one who needed recovering, Lucia concluded when Luke shocked her by giving her a hug.

'Good job,' he said, springing back.

'What did you do that for?' she gasped.

'No particular reason,' Luke insisted on his way out of the room.

She was instantly suspicious. The only time her brothers hugged her was when they were worried about her—if she had fallen off a horse, or something similar. It was their way of showing relief that she was okay, she supposed. So was Luke reassuring her that they could still be friends?

There was no point wishing for anything more, she told herself firmly as she returned to battle with the staples.

It was no use. They wouldn't budge. She would just have to take her uniform off.

'Margaret says the food is…' Luke's voice died as she dived behind the door.

Tired of greying white granny pants, she had treated herself to some new underwear in town—a gaudy display of shocking-pink lace to cheer her up when she was wearing work clothes. 'You're not supposed to be here,' she pointed out, cheeks glowing red when Luke showed no sign of leaving.

'Clearly…'

She held her breath while Luke and his sexy swagger finally returned to the kitchen.

'What *now*?' she exclaimed, feeling horribly caught out when he came back again.

'For goodness' sake, Lucia, I *have* seen you in a swimming costume before,' he pointed out impatiently, advancing on her with a pair of pliers.

Agreed. Luke *had* seen her half-naked before—when she was about sixteen. And she had been wearing a bikini at the time, which was somehow different. 'How did you know I was stuck to the stool?'

'Is that a serious question?'

Having freed the stool, Luke set it aside. 'Stick to what you do best in future. No one can do everything. Not even you, Lucia. Are there any more little jobs I can do for you before I go?'

Was *that* a serious question? 'You're going already?'

'To eat,' Luke's eyes darkened with amusement. 'Oh—and, Lucia?'

'Yes?'

'Nice underwear.'

Oh-kay.

'We shouldn't keep Margaret waiting,' he prompted, holding the door.

'I'll be right there.'

Just as soon as her heart had steadied.

She hesitated outside the kitchen door and then grasped the nettle. 'Beer?' she said casually, walking in. Luke was already seated at the head of the table, she noticed, bridling.

'Sweetheart, beer is *always* good.'

'What have I told you?' she warned him on her way across the kitchen.

'I promise never to call you sweetheart again.'

She glanced over her shoulder at Luke. His face was straight enough, but his eyes were dancing with laughter. She reached for a glass.

'Can I help you do that?'

She inhaled sharply to find him at her side. *Damn.* Luke moved like a soft-pawed predator. 'I can reach, thank you.'

'I don't need a glass.'

'Then what *do* you want?' she asked breathlessly.

Luke's mouth was very close to her ear, and although if anyone could make her lose her fear of men it was probably Luke, no way would she put that theory to the test.

'Maybe I need to practise my bar skills on someone,' she suggested, pulling away.

'Practise away,' he said, shooting her one last thoughtful look.

Still none the wiser as to what Luke had been up to in London, she decided to concentrate on being a consummate professional—something tangible within her reach. Thanks to Margaret's excellent cooking she served the perfect meal. She served the perfect coffee too, and Luke was pleased.

'If you continue like this you'll have the place full in no time,' he told Margaret. 'That was delicious, thank you. I'll take a look around now, and check out what's got to be done about the décor and furnishings—'

'That's my department,' Lucia interrupted.

'Says…?' Luke's gaze narrowed.

'Says me,' Margaret confirmed. 'That's what Lucia and I have agreed.'

'Oh, have you?' Luke smiled at Margaret, but reserved another look entirely for Lucia.

The challenge made her stare him down—or attempt to. Then Luke stood and the sizeable farmhouse kitchen shrank around him. For a moment she wondered if he was going to thump the table and roar that no one decided who did what unless *he* signed it off.

'Perhaps you two could check out the place together,' Margaret suggested tactfully as the atmosphere in the kitchen took a dive. 'I've asked Lucia to be my manager,' she explained, as evenly as if she were pointing out the fact that Lucia's new bucket and mop set was in a nicer shade of blue. 'And Lucia has agreed. Isn't that wonderful, Luke?'

'We'll discuss this later,' Luke managed through gritted teeth.

'Would you like to follow me?' Lucia asked mildly.

'No, I'll lead the way,' Luke insisted. 'Having stayed here for at least ten consecutive years I'm sure I don't need anyone to lead me round.'

Message received loud and clear. But she led the way anyway.

'What the hell is this nonsense about you being manager?' Luke demanded the moment the door had closed on Margaret.

'How much experience of running a hotel do you have, Luke?' Lucia challenged. 'Exactly,' she said when a muscle in his jaw worked. 'You've got more money than Croesus, as well as endless experience in the international business arena, but I have the hands-on experience—which began around the time Nacho asked me if I could organise a polo supper for him. I think I was about fourteen at the time. Plus, I fully understand that you need to be sure your investment in the Sundowner is safe, but let neither of us fool ourselves. I know this place is a means to an end for you. You want to reinstate Polo on the Beach and the Sundowner Guest House is in the perfect position: perfect stables, perfect access to the beach—'

'You seem to have it all worked out,' Luke growled tensely.

'Let's just say I'm not the child you seem to think I am. Shall we start the tour?'

'It seems I don't have much option but to go along with this for now, as Margaret has already appointed you.'

'Not so much of the "for now",' she warned. 'I fully expect to be fired if I fall short in any way. But the one thing I don't need is for you to prop me up.'

'You'd just like to spend my money?' Luke suggested coolly.

'Margaret appreciates your investment,' Lucia countered pleasantly. 'Shall we?' she suggested.

Luke's eyes flashed a warning signal that clearly stated it was game on. 'After you,' he bit out.

CHAPTER ELEVEN

Fans self... Hot momma, this man might not be mine
but I cannot—will not—think about anyone else making a move on him. I might be damaged goods, but I'm
still capable of admiring a fine uss. And in the unlikely
event that Luke ever made a serious move on me I can
rest assured that it could never come to anything because he'd soon realise that when it comes to sex I'm a
complete non-starter. So when he finally settles down I
shall just have to go on retreat to Outer Mongolia and
never come back...

FOR the sake of maintaining a professional front she blanked
Luke, huge and powerful, dwarfing her completely as he
stayed close at her side as they went up the stairs. Luke in
snug-fitting jeans—a little frayed, a little ripped, a little pale
and worn in places. She refused to notice that too. Inviting
him to go ahead of her at one point, she surveyed the tight hips
and muscular thighs—purely out of clinical interest, of course.
Just as she'd thought. He was bigger than her brothers. And
that heavy Aran sweater did look great with Luke's swarthy
skin, his hunky build and brooding amber gaze.

And there it ended, Lucia told herself firmly. Luke Forster
would be the first to admit that he believed women existed to
be protected, rather than to stick their heads above the para-

pet and invade a man's world. Women were far better seen and not heard—preferably in the bedroom, she imagined, remembering the blonde.

'You're being uncommonly accommodating, Lucia,' Luke commented as she led the way down the landing.

'I'd like to show you the attic room,' she replied in a businesslike tone, careful to maintain distance between them.

'I'm all attention,' Luke said, moving close enough for their hands to brush.

She led him into the huge room that took up much of the top of the house. It had the most spectacular view through picture windows of the endless beach and the sea beyond. Margaret had always dreamed of turning it into a residents' lounge and library. Lucia explained this to Luke. The room was still full of ladders and decorating equipment, but she threaded her way through all the tackle until she reached the windows where they could look out over a beach the colour of rich Jersey cream and the wild Cornish sea beyond, which had turned from angry pewter to smooth, crystalline blue.

'What do you think?'

'Apart from the shock of discovering Margaret has appointed you manager of the Sundowner, do you mean?' Luke enquired, hitting her with a curve ball.

'I imagine you could override that if you wanted to,' she said, returning to the subject at hand. 'So, what do you think?'

'You know what I think,' Luke growled. 'I love this place. But to turn it into an exclusive venue for international polo players who are used to the best will be a complex project.'

'And you don't think I'm up to it?'

'You're not exactly tried and tested.'

Wasn't that the truth? And now she must stick to the subject at hand. 'I'm not an amateur, either,' she said. 'I may not have your facility for figures and keeping ten thousand plates spinning at once, but I do know how to run a hotel—and from the bottom up. I can stand in for any job you care to name.'

Except for one, he thought, remembering the concierge.

'And if anyone knows how to cater for demanding polo players,' she pointed out, 'it's me.'

He couldn't argue with that. 'So, how do you feel about us working together, Lucia?'

'How do *you* feel about it?' she countered.

As if it was going to be difficult to concentrate, he concluded, feeling his groin tighten as Lucia continued to stare at him. This was not the girl from the beach, or from the wedding. This was a woman who had been through a lot since he'd last really known her, and who had gained in strength because of it. It made Lucia a better fit with the job, and made his life a lot more interesting.

'Can you cope with my being your boss?'

Her eyes flared and then she relaxed, seeing his eyes smiling into hers. 'So long as I don't have to bow and scrape,' she said.

'I'll put a clause in your contract to that effect,' he offered dryly. 'So…?'

'So Margaret is thrilled by your investment,' she said carefully. 'Just so long as you understand that my life isn't on the agenda, Luke. I refuse to live my life by committee a moment longer.'

'I think I've gathered that.'

'Well,' she said, 'if that's it…? I hope you like the changes I'm making.'

'Why don't I take a look?' he said.

It soon became apparent that Lucia had touched things with fairy dust. Even on Margaret's limited budget the old house was already being brought up to scratch, with hours of work having been put in—by Lucia, he imagined. There were quirky touches only she could have dreamed up—driftwood from the beach arranged to look like a piece of art on a high ledge, where it cast intriguing shadows on the pale chalky walls, and bleached wooden chairs upholstered in faded blue ticking inviting relaxation in a tranquil reading room, where the only ornament was a bowl of fresh flowers set in the centre of a vast refectory table on which newspapers could be laid out flat, or books studied in the natural light of the panoramic window framing the shore.

He paused at the window to stare out at a sky rapidly changing from daytime shades of smoky-blue to a cloak of night, streaked with red-gold.

'Luke?'

He turned to see Lucia standing waiting for him in the doorway. 'You're a real homemaker, Lucia.'

'There's no need to sound so surprised,' she said, smiling. 'Anyway, if you want to linger and soak up the view I just thought I should let you know I'm going out.'

'Okay.' He ground his jaw as he listened to her footsteps fading. She couldn't spare five more minutes to talk to him? And where was she going? he wondered as the front door opened.

To the beach.

He might have known. He watched until her shadow had disappeared down the cliff path and then pulled away from the window.

She was endlessly fascinated by the busy little creatures darting about the rock pool so purposefully in their unknowable lives. Hugging herself, she leaned her chin on her knees to watch them.

'Lucia...'

She glanced around, even though she knew her mother couldn't be calling her. Demelza Acosta was long dead, so she could hardly be running across the beach towards Lucia, trailing one of those big straw hats she'd used to love, her long red hair blowing wild and free in the fickle Cornish breeze. But if Lucia closed her eyes she could almost see her mother— barefoot and laughing, calling out as she came closer for Lucia to run with her. She'd be wearing one of those dresses that were totally unsuitable for the beach. It would be long and flowing, with a dainty flower print, and would keep catching round her mother's legs. Her mother would laugh all the more as she struggled to free herself, and when she finally made it to the rock pool she would grab hold of Lucia's hand and take her running, which often meant dodging the boys on their horses. Her mother had loved that game. She'd said tempting fate was exciting.

The dream ended abruptly, because Lucia hated giving in to weakness. She preferred to laugh and make jokes.

'Lucia?'

She glanced up in surprise to find Luke watching her. 'I didn't hear you. The wind,' she explained briskly, knuckling her eyes.

'Sorry if I'm intruding,' he said, shifting position. 'I just wanted to find you and say what a wonderful job you've been doing at the guest house.'

'I'm glad you approve,' she said, putting on her flippant voice. She felt vulnerable and exposed after her emotional workout. She braced herself and stood to face Luke.

'You're not going yet, are you?' he said as she glanced at the cliff path.

'It's getting cold.'

'Have I done something to upset you?' Luke probed.

'Oh, you know,' she said, reverting to the old mocking tone.

'No, I *don't* know,' Luke said, frowning. 'I'd like you to explain. What are you running away from, Lucia?'

She drew in a fast breath as Luke took hold of her arm. 'Nothing,' she said edgily. 'I just want to go back.'

Luke lifted his hands away. 'If that's what you want.'

'If you've come looking for the past, you won't find it here,' she blurted out. 'Sorry.' She tried a laugh that didn't quite work. 'Don't know where *that* came from,' she added in a jokey voice, pulling a face.

He did. 'I always come to the beach when I want to recapture those feelings from years back. There's nothing wrong with that, Lucia—'

'I tried it,' she interrupted. 'And it doesn't work for me. I've looked for the past here, but I can't find it.'

As emotion welled behind her eyes she stared away to sea. Lucia couldn't see her handsome Argentinian father and her Cornish mother laughing together as they strolled along the beach as she had hoped, he guessed. All she had found in St Oswalds was a rundown guest house and an old lady battling to keep things afloat without any real hope of doing so. But he'd seen real prospects for change here, and found it hard to believe Lucia couldn't see how large a part she played in that. Her confidence must have taken a real kicking. And now he knew why and how. He just had to be sure he got the timing to voice his concerns and got the healing absolutely right.

'The worst thing of all,' she said, distracting him, 'was that until you came along I couldn't see how I could help.'

'You've already helped Margaret with your friendship and with your company, as well as your hard work. And we're not finished yet,' he assured her.

'It's all words, Luke.'

'No, it's not,' he argued. 'Let me prove it to you?'

'What do you mean?' she said, staring at him suspiciously, but there was just the ghost of remembered humour in her eyes and that was enough for him.

'Okay, here's the challenge,' he said. 'If I don't make you laugh and remember the good times we used to have on this beach I'll give you a wage-rise. How about that?'

'I haven't even fixed a wage with you yet,' she pointed out.

'So I've got nothing to lose.'

'You are totally shameless,' she protested.

Maybe he was, but she hadn't said no, and to see that smile still playing round her lips was enough for him.

'Luke, what are you doing?' Luke was kicking off his boots. 'Are you completely mad?' she demanded as he started unzipping his jeans. 'You can't be thinking of swimming in the sea. It's freezing! You *are* mad,' she concluded, backing away from the latest massive roller.

'Chicken?' Luke shouted back.

'Certainly not.' Well, maybe a little, she conceded as Luke started on his boxers.

She clutched the back of her head as Luke casually stripped them off. 'Luke, you can't do that! What if someone sees you?'

'You mean there are more people as mad as us?'

Swimming off a freezing cold beach at night? Hmm...

It wasn't like they hadn't done it before...

Oh, what the hell!

She was probably going to land herself with the most graphic erotic dream yet, but chicken she was not, Lucia concluded as Luke plunged into the sea. And, yes, he *was* tanned all over.

Shaking his head like an angry wolf, Luke roared back at her over the crash of surf, 'I thought you said we were equal, Lucia? Looks to me like I'm the superior being after all.'

Firming her jaw, she yelled, 'Turn your back.'

'You speak and I obey.'

'I wish,' Lucia muttered, tugging off her clothes.

She raced into the sea, shrieking and wailing as a wall of ice-cold water hit her. 'You didn't turn around,' she complained, regaining her feet. 'That shows blatant disregard of the rules.'

As if Luke cared. He was standing taking lazy inventory,

with his massive fists planted on his taut naked hips. The only thing she had to be grateful about was the fact that the sea at night provided them both with a modesty curtain. He dodged the spray as she shrieked a war cry and launched herself at him.

'Two can play at that game,' Luke confirmed.

Unfortunately it was yet another game at which Luke excelled.

'Okay, I give up,' she conceded, raising her hands in the air. 'You win!' she exclaimed, her voice shaking with tension as Luke towered over her.

'Do I?' he said, taking a firm grip of her arms. 'What's my prize?'

If she could draw breath to speak she might come up with something, but with the entire length of Luke's hot, magnificent body pressed up against hers it was hard to think, let alone speak.

'Warm now?' he murmured, dragging her closer still.

There was too much information bombarding her brain for her to spare breath for an answer. But feeling more of Luke than was safe, she pulled away.

'You still don't trust me?'

Her answer was to place her hands flat against his chest in an involuntary defensive action.

'Dry yourself, Lucia. Get dressed and then we'll talk,' Luke said crisply as he turned to stalk back through the waves to the shore. Having snatched up his jeans and stepped into them, he strode away in the direction of the guest house. 'You were right about this place,' he called back. 'There's nothing here but sea and rock and sand.'

'Luke, wait.' Tying her shirt in a knot around her waist and wearing her jeans like a shawl, she chased after him. Managing finally to catch up, she grabbed hold of his arm.

'Don't let me spoil things for you. I was in a dark place tonight—it's nothing, just a phase.'

'Take care it doesn't become a way of life,' he said, shaking her off.

Luke was frighteningly right with that remark, Lucia realised, gritting her teeth as she ran after him. 'Margaret's out late with her friend, the farmer from across the road,' she explained, skipping backwards as she spoke. She was desperate for a return to normality between them. How would she work with Luke otherwise?

'So?' he demanded, still striding on, refusing to look at her.

It was a relief when he walked past the car. 'So come to the house,' she said. 'Take a shower—put some dry clothes on. We can have something hot to drink. We'll soon warm up.'

He stopped so abruptly she almost cannoned into him. 'How long are you going to pretend that this is all about whether you're cold or I'm cold, or if there are ghosts on the beach, Lucia? You must know I had to find out what happened in London. You must know I couldn't leave it without knowing what you were running away from.'

She flinched at his choice of words. 'What are you saying?' Ice washed through her. She couldn't read Luke's expression. She only knew he was saying horribly hurtful things she had been doing her best to avoid—true things—events she couldn't face any more than she could face the cold expression in Luke's eyes.

'I'm saying that I found out for myself what you didn't trust me enough to tell me, Lucia.'

'Luke—'

'I'll make a bargain with you, and my bargain is this,' he said, speaking over her. 'We talk about the past. We don't hide things from each other. And you don't hide your tears from me. Stop,' he added grimly when she tried to protest. 'I don't want to hear your jokes or your excuses. What happened to you in London is too serious for that.'

'I know. I told the police.'

'So you told the police but you couldn't tell me?'

'I told them as soon as Margaret told me you were in London, but I guess you got there first.'

'I guess I did,' Luke agreed. 'What, Lucia?' he demanded fiercely, grabbing hold of her. 'How could you imagine I would think any less of you because of what happened in London? I only wish you'd told me.'

'I…' She couldn't find the words as she stared up into Luke's complex expression. There was anger in his eyes— hurt too—but most of all there was the strength she should have remembered was always there.

'Those were great days on this beach, Lucia. There's no shame in remembering them with laughter, and even with tears. I don't see how either of us can come here without feeling something, and I don't want you to shut me out. The past belongs to both of us. Can't you see that?'

She heaved a great shuddering breath, knowing she must find the strength to tell Luke exactly what had happened in London. He was right that the past had to be faced up to and dealt with.

'Do you remember that barbecue?' he murmured, so softly she barely heard him.

'How could I forget?'

She knew exactly the day he was referring to. As Luke turned to stare at the spot where their two families had gathered she took the chance to pull on her clothes. By the time Luke turned around his face had softened and all the anger was gone.

'My brothers nearly set fire to the table,' she said, remembering.

'The table my mother insisted must be brought down from

the guest house, complete with linen tablecloth, silver table settings and candlesticks,' Luke supplied.

'My mother burnt the food.' She began to smile.

'But your father saved the day,' Luke pointed out.

'Your father helped,' she reminded him. 'They really liked each other, didn't they?'

'Strangely, they did,' Luke agreed, remembering his stiff, unbending father forming a surprisingly easy relationship with Lucia's striking, autocratic father.

'Not sure our mothers got on so well,' she said, 'though they always made the effort—'

'Both of them were polite to a fault,' Luke cut in, 'though there was never going to be too much common ground between them,' he admitted, thinking back. His mother had always been too worried about what people might think, while Lucia's mother hadn't given a damn.

'They were good days,' she said quietly.

'Yes, they were,' he agreed, shifting position to shield her from the wind. 'You'd better get back to the house.'

Luke wanted space—just as she did sometimes, Lucia guessed, taking the hint. 'I'll head in and grab the first shower,' she said.

'Were you crying when I first came down to the beach?' Luke probed softly, returning to the subject uppermost in his mind.

'I should have remembered you're the master of waiting until you're certain your dart will strike home.' Her mouth pulled in a rueful line.

'That wind can be a real nuisance sometimes,' Luke commented, but his eyes were warm with concern.

'Yes, it can be,' she agreed, holding his gaze steadily.

He caught hold of her as she went to move past him. 'So, do we have a bargain?' he demanded, staring into her eyes.

'A bargain not to hide our feelings about the past from each other?'

'All right… Yes, we do.' She couldn't pretend she wasn't disappointed that that seemed to be the only thing on Luke's mind.

Lifting his hands away from her, he let her go. 'Margaret's been talking about a party for everyone involved in the restoration of the guest house. Have you heard anything about it, Lucia?'

'Yes,' she admitted. 'Will you be here for it?'

'I'll do my best.'

Hurt, she demanded, 'How low down on your list are we?'

'Not low enough,' Luke growled.

When he yanked her close this time she was expecting some sort of lecture, but that was the last thing Luke had in mind. All thoughts of Luke the friend, Luke the almost-brother, shot out of her head, to be replaced by Luke the man she had watched over the years growing into a formidable warrior, protector, leader, unofficial guardian angel. And, whether she wanted him in the past or not, pain-in-the-neck adviser. And unashamed sexual tiger, she was now forced to add to that list.

As emotion overwhelmed her she clung to him, standing on tiptoe to kiss him back. Luke soothed as he stimulated, and claimed her for his own even as he set her free. But he knew everything there was to know about wild creatures, and that like the wildest and most wary of them all Lucia needed the ultimate coaxing, so even as her own passion grew Luke stepped back.

'The wind's blowing up again,' he pointed out. 'You should get back to the house before you catch cold, Lucia.'

His thoughts were always for others and not himself. 'Just one thing first.'

'Name it.'

'Equals?' She held out her hand to shake his.

'Agreed,' he said.

When he clasped Lucia's hand their heat mingled. Her eyes darkened and her lips parted to suck in air, but there was still too much reserve in her—and until he got past that...

She turned for home as if nothing of significance had passed between them.

But it had and they both knew it. They had both committed to travelling the same road together for a while, with neither of them certain where that road might lead. His goal had always been straightforward: restore St Oswalds and the guest house, and then shoot back to attend to his other business interests. But then he'd rediscovered Lucia and retraced her steps to London, with everything that involved.

He should have known life was always going to be more complicated than he had originally planned.

CHAPTER TWELVE

They say that you have to get all the pus out of a wound before it can heal, but the cleansing of the wound can be traumatic.

They say that what doesn't kill you makes you stronger.

Who is this indefatigable 'they'? And have 'they' tried it? Have 'they' tried laying themselves bare in front of the one person with whom 'they' least want to share their shame?

THEY reached the house and parted without a word to find a shower. She came down to find Luke in the kitchen. He didn't waste any time—but then subtlety had never been Luke's strong point.

'Let's talk about what happened in London,' he said tensely, his eyes like shards of glass.

'Luke, please, I don't want to do this now.' Her voice rose with every syllable. Luke's expression told her he hadn't just dug up part of her life she had been trying so hard to forget, he had laid it bare, and now he was going to shake it in her face and demand a reaction. 'Please don't make me...'

Luke slammed the door shut so there was no escape from the kitchen. Leaning back against it, he said in a deceptively soft voice, 'As someone who cares about you, Lucia, I think it's important that we do this.'

'I don't care what you think. I don't need you to fight my battles for me, Luke—'

'So I'm not supposed to care that I find you working as a cleaner in a trashy club?' he broke in. 'Or to notice that you're living in a barely habitable caravan in Cornwall, out of season on a rundown caravan park?'

'You're happy enough to work with me.'

'Margaret's known us long enough,' Luke said, refusing to rise. 'And I'm giving Margaret the benefit of the doubt. Perhaps she's on to something.'

'Let me out of the kitchen now, Luke. I don't want to talk about this.'

'If not now, when?' he demanded. 'You'll never be ready, Lucia. You keep everything locked inside you until it grows like a worm and eats you from the inside out. And I won't stand by and watch that happen.'

Luke was whip-fast as she tried to slip past him. She stared in fury at his fists planted either side of her face on the door. 'If co-operation's the key to working together you're not making a great start,' she fired back. 'First you go nosing about in London, and now you're trying to—'

'I'm trying to what?' he bit out.

She had been distracted by something else. 'You've been fighting,' she exclaimed under her breath. 'Luke, what have you done?' she asked faintly.

Pulling back, he studied his bruised knuckles. 'I've been hitching up caravans and moving rocks. What?' he demanded. 'Do you seriously think I'd beat up on some sad, disgusting little man? Is that why you think my knuckles are bruised?'

'So you know...' she whispered.

'Of course I know,' Luke confirmed. 'What I can't understand is why you didn't tell me.'

'Because whatever happened in London I've dealt with it. It's over and it will never happen again.'

'*Is* it over?' Luke said quietly.

As he spoke Luke lowered his arms and stepped away from the door, but this time she made no attempt to escape. Leaning back against the wall, she hugged herself for comfort as she remembered the day her life in London had come to an abrupt end.

'Moving from getting a good degree to my new life in London was supposed to be so different from the way it worked out—so straightforward.'

He could have told Lucia that nothing in life was straightforward, but he had waited so long for her to let the poison out he wasn't going to say a single word to distract her.

She felt the shame again—of arriving at the guest house feeling pretty much like the filthy slut the concierge had called her. She remembered how her heart had raced with fear and panic that Margaret might turn her away. She had realised how it must look to the elderly owner of the guest house, but Margaret had taken her in without a word.

'It all began when I went to change my uniform,' she explained to Luke. 'I went into the staffroom. I didn't bother locking the door. It was supposed to be for female members of staff. It was a very formal hotel in London, so I should have been safe. I heard a sound, and when I turned around a concierge I thought was my friend was standing by the door, watching me.'

She had to pause. She didn't want to make this overly dramatic. She wanted to remember it exactly as it had been without any theatrical flourishes.

She shuddered, remembering. 'He was touching himself through his trousers as he watched me getting changed. When I turned and he saw me looking at him he gave himself a special firm stroke. I couldn't believe it. You'd think he'd be embarrassed—but, no… He came closer while I stood frozen to the spot. My feet wouldn't work. He stood in front of me and asked in a really normal, conversational tone of voice if I would like to touch him. When I said no and shrank back, he said, "What? A hot-blooded South American like you doesn't want to touch *me*?" And I could tell he had taken offence.'

She swallowed and turned away from Luke as she remembered the violence the concierge had unleashed.

'He undid his zip and exposed himself. He asked if there was something wrong with him when I shrank away. His voice turned ugly.' The calm beam of Luke's stare remained on her face, willing her to go on. 'He was angry when I wouldn't take hold of him. Sorry—'

Spinning around, she gagged. Clamping her hand over her mouth as her stomach heaved, she moved away, her hand up to ward him off when Luke reached for her.

'Dry gagging's no fun,' she said, trying to make light of what had happened when her stomach settled.

Luke wasn't smiling.

She steadied her voice. 'He rubbed against me. I slapped him away. I fought him with everything I had. He turned rough. He was touching me everywhere. He felt my breasts. He hurt me. He bit me. He grabbed me here. He ripped my briefs off. He poked his—'

She couldn't go on. How could she, when she saw that look in Luke's eyes?

'Go on,' he encouraged steadily.

Heaving a deep breath, she made herself go back. 'I kicked him in the knee as hard as I could. While he was howling and lurching about I somehow managed to get away. I ran back to my room, grabbed my car keys and a few things. I didn't stop to wash.'

Her eyes when they met his were wounded, tortured.

'My skin was hot. I was sure he'd put something on it—

acid or something. Of course it was nothing. Just the imprint of his hands. I got down to my car—they let us park under the hotel—and I drove out of London. I didn't even know where I was going until I reached Exeter, and then I knew I was heading back to the guest house where I'd always been happy.' She swallowed on a dry throat. 'I couldn't go to the family penthouse in London. My brothers could have turned up at any time and they were the last people I wanted to see.'

'Thank goodness Margaret was home.'

'Yes,' she agreed, finally focusing on his face. 'But I must have frightened Margaret half to death. She opened the door to a madwoman with her hair sticking out at all angles, make-up smeared with tears, ripped clothes hanging off a body covered in bite marks and scratches. I can't even imagine how she must have felt when she saw me.'

He could.

There was a long pause as she remembered that first bliss-ful, purging shower, and how she had examined her skin in minute detail under the spray, certain the concierge had put something horrible on it—something she would never be able to wash off. She had stood beneath that cleansing stream, scrubbing herself with the roughest cloth she could find until the water ran cold.

'Lucia…'

'I'm sorry.' She lifted her hands and let them drop again, by which time some warmth was creeping back into her body. 'That's all there is,' she said.

'It's enough,' Luke said gently.

'Sleeping with that concierge would have really opened my eyes, apparently.' She tried to laugh, but even to her it didn't sound right. 'And my legs, presumably, which was the bit that really freaked me out.'

This time when Luke gathered her into his arms she made no attempt to fight him off. 'Why didn't you call *me*?' he said, nuzzling his face against the top of her head. 'I would have come for you right away.'

'I felt so ashamed, so dirty. It wasn't something I wanted anyone to know. And it was my problem.'

'Not this time, Lucia,' he said, pressing her against his chest, where she could feel Luke's heart beating, regular and strong.

'It was better you didn't know,' she argued. 'You might have killed someone.'

'Quite possibly,' Luke confirmed, staring grimly away. Then, slowly and very deliberately, he dipped his head and kissed her. She couldn't say whether that kiss was soothing or loving, long or short, firm or light. She only knew that she was in a place where people were kind to each other and only meant well.

'Forgive me, Lucia,' he said, pulling back. 'That's the last thing you need.'

'It's everything I need,' she argued. 'I should have known you wouldn't rest until you found out what had happened in London. I think you and my brothers are throwbacks to some warrior race, where honour is a badge worth fighting to the death for.'

'And where those warriors believe that little girls never grow up?' he suggested gently.

'You're all guilty of that,' she agreed. 'But I can assure you this girl's all grown up.' She gave Luke's chest a half-hearted thump as she pulled away.

'Come back here.'

'Let me go, Luke,' she said, trying to be firm with him. 'I'm warning you.'

'No, you're not,' he argued gently. 'You're resting on me, because that's what you've always done when you're upset. You know you can tell me anything. You always could.'

'In the absence of anyone else to confide in,' she admitted ruefully.

'You always did know how to make me feel valued,' he teased her gently.

'You *are* valued,' she said, staring up into his eyes. 'You have no idea.'

He was all out of words.

Her mind crashed as Luke's mouth covered hers. She gave a whimper and, hearing his responding growl, shivered with the relief of a wounded animal being rescued by its mate. Luke cupped her head in one big hand as he moved his lips against hers, and kissing him back was like coming home. She had never been frightened of Luke. He might look like a barbarian—he might even act like one on the polo field—but Luke was her lodestone, her rock. She just hadn't ever risked thinking of him as a man who might want her after what had happened. And if he'd leave it at kisses...

Luke sensed the change in her immediately and pulled back.

'Why?' she whispered.

'Because you're not ready,' he said, staring deep into her eyes. 'And this is not the time.'

He left her to go and get his jacket, which he'd hung on the coat stand in the hall. He was smiling as he brought a small package back with him. 'I almost forgot this.'

'What is it?'

'I bought you something.'

'Something else?' she said wryly, her lips pressed in a questioning line.

'I don't like buying gifts from hotels,' Luke explained. 'It always feels like the easy option to me. And, okay, it *was* the easy option,' he admitted. 'Nacho asked me to buy you something. So this is from me. I found it in London. I hope you like it. Happy birthday, Lucia.'

She smiled when she saw what the elegantly packaged gift-box contained. 'Are you telling me I need to brush my hair?' she said as she examined the exquisitely crafted hairbrush.

'I rather thought I might do it,' he murmured.

'Luke, it's beautiful. I love it.'

The back of the brush was enamelled in turquoise lacquer decorated with intricate whorls in soft gold and rose-pink. The craftsmanship was so fine it took her breath away. That and the prospect of Luke brushing her hair, which was a fantasy yet to be explored and far more erotic than anything she might have dreamed up.

'You shouldn't do this,' she said, shaking herself round. 'It must have cost you a fortune.'

Luke shrugged. 'I can always take it back.'

She hugged it close. 'Not a chance.'

'Well, I'd better be going.'

Luke tugged on his jacket as if nothing unusual had happened between them, while she felt as if everything had changed. 'Goodnight, Luke.'

His hand warmed her arm briefly as she opened the door, and then he walked past without another word.

Oh, well. Closing the door behind him, she leaned back against the polished wood, trying to fathom out whether all her painful revelations had brought them closer together or pushed them further apart.

Luke didn't trust himself to stay a moment longer. He had wanted to grab hold of Lucia and hold her tight and safe for ever. It had taken all the will power he possessed to leave her at the door. Whatever she thought of him, he respected her bid for freedom and her need for time to put what had happened in London behind her. But she had smelled so good—so fresh and innocent. She had aroused every protective instinct in him. And, on the dark side, he wasn't nearly done with kissing her yet.

Or with giving her gifts, Luke reflected as he climbed into his car.

It was ironic to think that Lucia had always been the risk-taker while he considered every move. Events in London had changed them both for ever, turning the world as they knew it onto its head. It would be some time before Lucia could trust a man again, and he had been so sure his soulmate would be a soothing, peaceful, calming beauty—no drama, no temperament, no ruffles in the smooth waters of his life.

When he reached the Grand his head was still full of Lucia. He stormed into his suite, took another shower and dried off. Dressing quickly, he told himself not to be so rash, and that work was the answer. Raking his damp hair impatiently, he crossed to the desk and tried to focus on a line of figures Lucia had asked him to look at. They blurred into her lovely face. Anger followed at the thought of the pain she had suffered when he hadn't been there to stop it.

With a violent curse, he slammed the lid down on his laptop. 'Crazy!' he exclaimed. She made him laugh. She made him lust. She made him throw up his hands in exasperation.

He realised he hadn't known a moment's peace since his first day in St Oswalds, when he had spotted a wild and lovely young girl on the beach. He'd never seen anything like Lucia before. To him she had seemed like some exotic bird in comparison with the tame canaries back home. There hadn't been a day since then when he hadn't thought about her.

Lucia's family had been too busy with their own concerns to notice the tightrope she was walking, but he had.

And now she didn't need him. How did that feel?

It stuck in his craw.

CHAPTER THIRTEEN

Get a wax

Luke is right. I have to move on. No wonder he gave up and walked out on me. When did I turn into such a wuss? Picking up my old to-do list, I scoured it. Apart from more serious matters, what else have I been avoiding?

Oh, yes.

I drew a blank with the fast search company on the phone—maybe I wasn't frank enough with the man on the other end of the line? Thankfully my chat with Grace from the club bore fruit. Not only will I not have to brave the chi-chi beauticians at the Grand and risk running into Luke, which would be embarrassing to say the least, but apparently there is a new place, a local place, a small and discreet place, tucked away in the backstreets of St Oswalds.

And, bonus! If the stress of what I am about to do gets too much for me, the salon also offers massage by Britain's strongest woman.

Banker's Bonus: I have managed to score their last appointment.

THE lights were pink neon; the windows were obscured glass. The words 'Power Massage' plastered over a banner didn't exactly instil confidence in a girl who believed in preserving her body by never using it. But she wasn't here for a massage, Lucia reassured herself as she opened the door.

'Veruschka will be with you in a moment,' the receptionist in the well-packed white uniform purred, staring up through a fringe of false black lashes as if she could read Lucia's fear and knew she was dreading it. 'Veruschka is *verrry* good… *verrry* gentle…'

Eek.

The door to the back room creaked open.

But it was only a really nice young girl, around Lucia's age, with a high ponytail, hardly any make-up and a nice clean shirt and jeans.

'Come this way, please,' she said with a friendly smile.

Oh, this wasn't going to be at all bad. What on earth had she been worried about?

Okay, so this might be a bit of a problem, Lucia conceded, holding up the paper thong when the girl had left her in the dressing room. Not that she hadn't seen a thong before, but as the thin bit was at the back and the waxing wasn't, which way round should she wear it?

Never mind. They'd given her a gown, and that nice girl would soon put her right if she'd got it wrong. 'Veruschka…? I'm ready…'

'This way, please.'

Had Veruschka turned into a man?

That wasn't a young girl's voice, Lucia reasoned, hovering nervously behind the plastic curtain.

She gasped as the curtain was ripped aside and a woman as tall as her brothers and at least as wide stood, beefy arms akimbo, waiting for her. 'I am Veruschka,' the Titan informed her.

'I'm not here for a massage,' Lucia explained in a shaking voice.

'No,' the woman said in *basso profundo*. 'You are here for waxing.'

'Correct.' Dropping her shoulders, Lucia lifted her chin. Wasn't this a rigmarole women the world over put up with? Was she less than the rest? Was she a wuss?

Yes.

She was lying prone and stiff on the hard, plastic-covered couch, just wondering how to broach the subject of the thong, when Veruschka turned.

'We start with the moustache and then we move on to the big guns.'

What?

'Oh, good... Perhaps...'

Too late. The pot, the Titan and the red-hot wax were on their way.

The wax cooled rapidly. So far so good—though she hadn't realised her moustache covered half her face before. And...

Youch!

Was it supposed to hurt so much?

'Tell you what, Veruschka. Shall we leave it there?'

She didn't wait for an answer. By the time Veruschka thundered something in reply Lucia was already in the changing cubicle, tugging on her jeans.

'Just take it,' she said, thrusting money at the dazed receptionist. 'No—no change. And definitely no vouchers for a return visit,' she insisted, waving them away.

Get a cool new wardrobe.

It wasn't all lose-lose. Now she had made a start on her to-do list another item followed swiftly on the heels of the wax. It was late-night shopping in town—the perfect opportunity to choose a couple of smart suits for when the guest house was finished and she was front of house. Being given free rein was quite a novelty after the black suit or black suit choice she had had in London. And she could put something fairly nice together without spending too much money if she shopped around…

This was so ridiculous she couldn't believe she was doing it—except it was something she felt compelled to do. It was almost dark and she was down on the beach, showing off her new outfits to her mother. She wanted her to see them. She was wearing one of her new suits—a smart, tailored navy blue number—teamed with a violet top underneath. One exclamation mark per outfit was enough, Lucia's mother had always told her.

The suit fitted Lucia like a glove. She had even had to go down a size. Not that she was back to her old self yet—far from it—but with high heels on she didn't look half bad.

'Just a minute,' she said, teetering about as first one and then the other heel sank into the sand. 'There,' she murmured, imagining her mother watching her. 'What do you think?' she said, slowly turning in a circle.

'I think you look amazing…'

She nearly jumped out of her skin. 'Luke!'

'Who else were you talking to?'

She laughed a little nervously. This wasn't the time to admit she had been communing with her long-dead mother. 'You really think so?' she said, frowning. 'You don't think the violet top is too much?'

'I think the colour combination is as unique as you, Lucia.'

Was that good or bad? she wondered wryly. She took a chance. 'I'm glad you approve.'

'Do you need me to steady you?' he asked, when she stood like a stork to take her shoes off.

'You'll never do that, Luke.'

Humour flashed across his eyes. 'It won't stop me trying.'

She rested one hand on the hard muscles of his upper arm. 'How did you know I'd be here?'

'Do you really need to ask that question?'

Luke was right. They had always been in tune with each other's thoughts. It was reassuring to know they still were—though not quite so reassuring to see the brooding look in his eyes, or to feel her body respond to it. Even she couldn't misinterpret the growing tension between them. And what if Luke wanted more than kisses?

'So?' she prompted brightly, shaking off her brush with apprehension. 'Are you thirsty? Do you want to come back to the house and have a coffee or a beer?'

'Lucia, stop babbling,' Luke advised, 'or you'll have me thinking I make you nervous.'

'As if,' she scoffed.

'Before I think about a drink,' he said, turning serious, 'I've drawn up some projected figures you should take a look at.'

'Oh…how interesting.' And now she felt flat, when surely she should be feeling relieved that Luke was only here to talk business rather than to make her confront more demons than she was ready for. 'Business comes first,' she agreed, starting up the packed sand path.

'You never did tell me what you're doing on the beach in a business suit, talking to yourself,' Luke remarked casually, strolling alongside her.

'That's right, I didn't,' she said, playing his game as she hurried on.

She was at the top of the cliff before she realised Luke wasn't following her. He was still down on the beach, watching the last blood-red rays of the sun sizzling and finally going out on a charcoal horizon.

The temperature had dropped suddenly, and a stiff wind was whipping his hair. He registered those things in some logical storage compartment in his mind while Lucia took up every other nook and cranny. How much time had they wasted?

Storming up the cliff path, he stopped dead at the top, seeing the guest house was in darkness. Where had she gone instead? He looked around wildly. There, to the left, he could see a light flickering in one of the windows of the caravan.

Jogging across the field, he stopped outside the door. There was a pause before anything happened, and then she finally wrenched the door open.

She smiled crookedly at him.

'You've been crying. Did you miss me?' His lips tugged at this suggestion.

'You're so full of it,' she said, but at least she was smiling again. 'As it happens, I'm jealous because Margaret's gorging herself on freshly churned butter and clotted cream with the farmer across the way. Are you coming in? Or do I have to stand here all night?'

'I can see the lack of clotted cream is as good a reason as any for your tears. I don't have any Cornish cream,' he said, brushing past her as he entered the van, 'but I can offer you some good, honest brawn, if that's any good?'

She gave him a look—eyes narrowed, chin up. 'You'll do, I suppose,' she said, pressing back against the side of the van to let him pass. 'You're impossible,' she murmured when he gave her a wry stare back.

And she was...*beautiful*. Her face was blotchy from crying, but that only made him want to hold her and make things right for her. 'So, come on, what's wrong?' he said briskly once the door was shut behind him.

'There's nothing's wrong,' she said, with a little too much heat.

'I don't buy that, Lucia.'

She bit down on her bottom lip, and her eyes were stormy

as she confronted him. 'Okay, so I was missing my mother,' she said angrily. 'Are you satisfied now?'

Reaching out, he brushed some tendrils of wayward hair from her face. 'Your mother would be very proud of you.'

'Do you really think so?'

'I know so. Margaret's been wearing my ears out telling me how hard you work, how great your ideas are, what a flair you have for the hospitality industry and how she can't think how she ever managed without you. Damn, this bed's uncomfortable,' he said, hunkering down on the edge of the narrow bunk. 'How the hell do you sleep here?'

'My room's nearly ready at the guest house, and this guy I know sent me some excellent throws and pillows.'

'Is this guy anyone I know?'

Scooping up a pillow, she chucked it at him. 'Does that help jog your memory?'

'There's only one thing that can help me.' Reaching out, he took hold of her.

Still laughing, she shook him off. 'Let me go, you great oaf!' She shrieked as he brought her crashing down on the bed at his side. 'This isn't the hay barn, and I'm not a child to be manhandled,' she insisted—but without much heat.

Feeling the soft cushion of her breasts beneath his arm, he thought he would happily vouch for that.

'And if this is about that work you mentioned, I've clocked off.'

'So have I,' he assured her.

'So why are you here?'

'Well, I wouldn't call this work,' he said, taking in every adorable aspect of her face.

'Are you sure?' Sitting up, she looked at him comfortably sprawled on her bed. 'Are you sure I'm not just work for you, Luke?'

'How can you say that?'

'I just have to look at your track record to date. You come. You go. You report back to my brothers, who tighten the reins until I squeak. Isn't that how it goes? Or has your role in my life changed?'

'My being here now has nothing at all to do with your brothers,' he assured her.

'Good, because when you see them you can tell them I've found something worth finishing, and I'm not going anywhere until I've done just that.'

'I'm not going anywhere, either.' He dragged her close.

'Luke, I—'

'You talk too much.' As he kissed her, he pushed the jacket down her arms and started on the buttons on her top.

'If this is one of your jokes...'

'This is not a joke, Lucia.' Her skin felt like warm silk beneath his hands, but there was still space between them, as if they both had to be sure. More than sure, they had to be certain.

'What are we doing?' she whispered.

'I'm making love to you.'

'Can we still be friends?' she asked, placing her hands flat against his chest in one final and not very convincing last-ditch attempt to hold him off.

'We'll probably argue more.'

'Impossible.'

He cut her off. Cupping her face in his hands, he kissed her tenderly and slowly. For a few seconds she resisted him, as if she didn't want to take the risk of damaging their friendship. In that moment he wondered if he'd called it wrong. He had never been uncertain in his life before, but where Lucia was concerned he was all over the place.

But just when he was about to pull back she softened against him and said, 'Again...'

'Why?' he demanded, smiling against her mouth. 'Did I get it wrong the first time?'

'I won't know until you kiss me again,' she said.

He dropped kisses on her mouth, teasing her, bringing her to a higher state of arousal, but he could sense that something still wasn't right. 'You know I'd never hurt you.'

'I know that.' She squirmed with embarrassment, and then turned her head so she didn't have to look at him as she admitted in a voice he could barely hear, 'There must be something wrong with me.'

'There's nothing wrong with you,' he insisted. 'Does this have something to do with London?'

'I don't want to talk about it, Luke.'

A bolt of fury hit him as the man who had done more damage than he knew flashed into his head. He was determined to prove to Lucia that fear had no place in her life, but before he could do anything she caught him off guard. He could only describe it as some dark side of Lucia taking her over. Locking her hands behind his neck, she dragged him down to kiss him with a fire that astounded him.

Seizing her wrists, he held her firmly beneath him, with her hands safely captured on the pillow above her head. He had never seen her like this, with her lips parted to suck in air, her eyes black with passion, but he needed no reminder that his reality did not include mindless sex with a woman he had loved since childhood.

'Lucia.' Having managed to free her hands, she had started tugging at his clothes. 'Lucia, stop that!' he said sharply.

Bringing her hands down, he held her as her expression changed from furious passion to shock at what she'd done, and then to something that stabbed at his heart, until finally she turned her face into the pillow as if she had done something wrong.

'Lucia, look at me,' he said gently. Drawing her into his

arms, he stroked her hair and kissed the top of her head. 'I only stopped you because it shouldn't be like this. Not the first time. Not for you.'

'But it isn't the first time,' she confessed, anguish at all her perceived faults making her voice break.

'I'm talking about the first time with *me*,' he said, his lips tugging wryly as he stared into her troubled eyes. 'If you really think I'm that sort of judgemental jerk, what are you doing in my arms?'

'Doesn't everyone think I'm a party girl?'

'Only those who can't see through you as I can.'

'I'm not like my mother, Luke.'

She made it sound like some sort of monumental failure, which really shocked him. He had never realised Lucia's insecurities cut so deep, or had such history.

'My mother was a free spirit, and I so wanted to be like her. But when I try to do the things she did I just make a mess of everything.'

'You don't make a mess of anything,' he argued tensely.

Lucia's mother had been more than a free spirit; she had been reckless. If Demelza Acosta hadn't insisted on going back into the *estancia* to save some silly trinkets Lucia's father wouldn't have tried to save her and they would both be alive today. He would never tell Lucia what he knew about the flood, but she was so wrong to compare herself unfavourably with her mother. Lucia had far more common sense.

He only realised now what coming back to Cornwall meant for both of them. It meant facing the truth—however unpalatable that truth might be.

'That concierge made me feel as if I'd led him on,' she said, pulling him back to the present with a jolt. 'I keep re-running what happened through my head to see if he was right, if it *was* my fault…'

'You've got to stop that right now,' he insisted pulling her into his arms. 'That man was sick. He was bad, Lucia. Look at me.' He cupped her chin with his hand so he could stare deep into her troubled eyes. 'What you're thinking is impossible. You would never act like that. I know for certain, because I know you better than anyone. You cover everything with humour and a bold face, but inside you're as tender as a—'

'Steak?' she suggested, reverting to the jokes that had always kept her safe before.

'I was thinking more tender as a summer night,' he said, lips tugging as she stared at him in disbelief.

'Since when has the Enforcer been a poet?' she demanded, narrowing her eyes.

'I went to school, too,' he said with a shrug.

Her gaze steadied on his as she realised that he had no intention of allowing her to distract him. She frowned, then heaved a breath and said, 'Okay. I worry that I can't…you know…' Turning her face away, she said, 'I can never give you what you want, Luke.'

The thought of some bully leaving her in this state made him angry all over again. 'Maybe I don't want as much as you think.'

'You just want kisses?' she said, pinning him with a suddenly fierce look. 'No. I didn't think so.'

It hurt to see her mouth twist in that heart-wrenchingly familiar grimace. From the day her parents had drowned, Lucia had hidden her feelings from everyone. She would rather tie her face in knots than let anyone see how she felt inside. That was the look she was giving him now.

'I'm not that bad, am I?' he said. 'You make me feel like Bluebeard.'

'It's not just the concierge and what he did to me,' she admitted. Drawing a deep breath, she went on, 'I've never—' She stopped. 'Help me out here.'

'Enjoyed sex?'

'How did you know I was going to say that?'

'I applied intuition,' he said dryly.

'What are you doing now?' she said as he tugged his top over his head.

'Equalling things up a bit,' he admitted.

'But my chest isn't naked,' she protested.

'Not yet.'

CHAPTER FOURTEEN

Get a great dance teacher
Right about now you're probably thinking, 'How can she be thinking about dance teachers at a time like this?'

Well, with the best dance teacher in the world currently holding me in Perfect Hold, I feel confident in this area of my life too.

Well, sort of...

LOVEMAKING started with kisses, strokes and whispers of endearment, and that much she could do.

The lightest brush of Luke's mouth sent pleasure jolting through her body. Her dreams had been full of this since the first day she'd seen him galloping flat out on the beach—though not as good as this...not nearly as good as this. And Luke proved to be the master of the outrageous suggestion, which aroused her even more.

She worried he wouldn't find her full figure sexy, but when Luke tossed her top aside her breasts fitted his big hands so perfectly that for the first time in her life she didn't wish them to be any different. There was such a connection between them she couldn't have summoned up a gram of fear even had she wanted to. Her only wish was to be closer and to sink deeper into incredible sensation, and then have it last for ever.

Lacing her fingers through Luke's hair, she kept him where

she wanted him as he dipped his head to tease her nipple with his mouth. Each tug of his lips brought a corresponding reaction of pleasure that throbbed insistently between her thighs. She loved the feel of strong sun-bleached waves springing against her palm, and the rasp of his stubble as he raised his chin to look at her.

Seeing the look in her eyes prompted him to move down the bed, while she writhed beneath him, wondering about nerve-endings that must have been sleeping but were now leaping into life. Unable to bear the frustration a moment longer, she undid the buttons at the waist of her suit trousers and slid them down.

Dark heat was burning in Lucia's eyes. Her hunger revealed itself in swollen lips and peaking nipples. Her inhibitions were lost in the need consuming her. All he wanted was for her to forget her fear, to be able to move past the block she had created in her mind to protect herself from the pain of what that man had done to her. He tasted innocence when he kissed her, which only made him all the more determined to protect her. He took time to enjoy the pleasures of her body. He drew deeply on the fragrance of her skin and revelled in her plump, smooth softness as she pressed herself against the hard, unyielding muscles of his chest.

'You're beautiful,' he murmured against her mouth.

'You have no idea what it took to get here.'

'Stop it,' he said gently. 'Stop with the jokes, Lucia. I mean it when I say you're beautiful. You've always been beautiful to me, and you're even more beautiful now.'

She gasped when Luke's hand touched her leg, but her eye contact with him didn't waver as he stroked and reassured, aroused and excited her—though she sucked in another fast breath when his hand reached her thigh. But Luke was in no rush, and now he teased her lips apart and her brain grew woolly. Stroking his tongue with hers was the greatest intimacy she had ever known with him, and as he deepened the kiss she welcomed the thrust of his thigh between her legs. She even angled herself in an attempt to catch more pleasure, but Luke was too clever for that, and always managed to keep just that little frustrating distance away. Breath gushed out of her in an excited sigh when he cupped her buttocks. The heat of those big rough hands was holding her so safely, even as they placed her in the most unimaginable danger.

Falling in love is dangerous.

'You're such a brute,' she murmured, making it sound like a compliment, which made him laugh.

Luke knew everything about delay and how it heightened pleasure. He knew she was swollen with need and that a pulse beat greedily at the heart of that need. But all he did was to cup her with one big hand, refusing to touch her where she wanted him to, almost as if he were stealing away her chance at pleasure.

'How can you?' she whispered heatedly, in an agony of desire. This was the worst frustration she had ever known. 'How *dare* you?' she complained when Luke just gave her that crooked smile.

'How dare I?' he said, lips tugging in amusement. And he kissed her with deadly efficiency and still held back.

'Luke…'

'What's the problem?' Luke murmured, lifting his head.

'You,' she said, biting down on swollen lips. 'Why must it be like this? Why make me wait so long?'

'Because pleasure should be savoured, and I want to make sure you are ready.'

As Luke said this she decided that if there was to be no reprieve she would take matters into her own hands, but her hands were shaking as she started to battle with the buckle on his belt. At least she had the satisfaction of knowing that Luke was massively erect, and by the time she managed to get her hands to the right place the zipper on his jeans didn't so much open as explode. Maybe he was right about taking things slowly.

He rested motionless while Lucia undressed him. She was right in that compared to her he *was* a brute. He was twice her size and goodness knew how much stronger, and as he bathed in the light of her clean, bright innocence he felt like a satyr on the loose. The thought that Lucia had never known true pleasure at the hands of a man made him doubly aroused, and doubly determined to serve and satisfy, but he would wait for as long as it took for Lucia to feel confident.

With this in mind he continued to lavish attention on her breasts with one hand, while his other rested motionless in place, denying her the quick fix she thought she wanted.

'Goodness, Luke,' she breathed.

He'd kicked his jeans off and she realised she had never seen him completely naked before—except in the sea, when it had been dark and the water had covered them both. He soothed her with words and kisses, giving her just a fraction more of the pressure she craved. As he did so her eyes opened wide with surprise and a breath shivered out of her.

Staring into his eyes, she managed to utter one word. *'More.'*

At the back of her pleasure-clouded mind she realised that she had been waiting for fear, but it didn't come. Instead a heavy, erotic beat pulsed urgently between her thighs. Luke still refused to take her any closer to the edge, as if he knew exactly where her limits lay. But when she got there would she be able to take that final step? Letting go meant trusting Luke completely.

'This can't be enough for you,' she said, already worrying.

'It isn't enough for *you*,' Luke countered wryly. 'Relax,' he said, moving down the bed.

This was all new to her, and she briefly resisted him slipping her legs over his shoulders. It made her feel so exposed. But the fight dissolved at the first touch of his tongue. And then the thought of Luke kneeling in front of her as he was doing now, to serve her and attend to her pleasure, was such an erotic notion she surrendered gladly and rested back.

'I want to see you come,' he said. Seeing her shocked expression, he added softly, with that humour in his eyes, 'Don't look so worried—there's no rush.'

Exhaling shakily, she settled back again, with her heart hammering so hard she could hardly breathe. Far from toning things down in deference to her inexperience, Luke slipped a pillow beneath her hips, exposing her even more as he positioned her in a way that suited him. Closing her eyes, she concentrated on sensation. The scratch of his sharp black stubble on the inside of her tender inner thigh was a thunderbolt to her senses.

'Look at me, Lucia.'

It was possibly the only time in her life that she had obeyed one of Luke's instructions without argument, but this time she did so willingly, and a cry shivered out of her as Luke's big hand turned into the most delicate instrument of pleasure. She couldn't hold back and screamed his name, while Luke made sure she enjoyed every second of the violent pleasure. The waves surging over her seemed never-ending, though at some point Luke must have collected her into his arms, because he was holding her safely now, as he kissed and stroked her until the last addictive ripple of enjoyment had subsided.

'Was that good?' he murmured.

'What do you think?' she managed, when she was capable of focusing on the world again.

But a new hunger soon started up inside her. She could feel Luke's erection pressing urgently against her thigh and was overwhelmed by the desire to have his tongue in her mouth, his pulsing energy deep inside her. The thought of them joined completely and in every way made her shiver with excitement.

'Greedy,' Luke murmured, though his hands were instantly at her service.

'Touch me,' she said.

'Touch *me*,' he challenged softly.

Closing her eyes, she reached for him and, stroking lightly, marvelled at the breadth of him, the incredible silken length.

'Again,' he said, 'and use more pressure this time.'

'What are you doing?' she asked, wondering if she had done something wrong when Luke broke away.

'I'm protecting us both. Help me?' he suggested.

Luke didn't have a shred of self-consciousness in him, and she fed on that. Involving her like this meant that nothing he did could come as a surprise to her. As if to confirm that, Luke dropped kisses on her mouth, and his eyes were smiling into hers with a new intimacy. This was a kiss between two people who had known each other for a lot longer than one night but who were seeing each other clearly for the first time.

A soft cry escaped her lips when somehow the tip of Luke's erection caught inside her. He was so intuitive, so tuned to her needs, that when he finally eased inside her she gasped with relief rather than fright. He rested, allowing her to become used to this new sensation, and it was she who moved again first—tentatively to begin with, and then with increasing confidence, until Luke took up the rhythm and she was mindless and free, completely free. No words could express how it felt to be one with Luke after so many years of loving him.

'You are my official sex slave now,' she informed him much later, when they were lying together on the bed with their limbs comfortably entwined.

'Do I get a contract to that effect?' he murmured, toying with her hair in between kissing her.

'An indefinite contract,' she assured him, drifting into sleep.

'Sounds good to me...'

When she woke Luke was still watching over her, with his face resting on the pillow next to hers. 'What?' she murmured when he smiled.

'You,' he said. 'At last.'

'What do you mean, me at last?'

'You, where you belong at last,' he said.

There were moments in life that were precious and would always be remembered, and this was one of them. This was the first time she had realised they both felt the same—for how long she couldn't know, since life had whipped them up and put them down in different places. But they were together now. And hungry again, she realised, seeing the smile tugging at the corner of Luke's mouth.

'No,' she said, deciding to tease him as he had teased her.

'That's fine by me,' he said, and laughed deep in his chest when she growled with frustration and threw herself on him.

He lost count of how many times Lucia had wanted him. He had never imagined she would be so passionate, or so insatiable. He would have loved her just the same without that, but it was a bonus.

Love?

Yes. Love. He had always loved Lucia. He just hadn't realised the extent of that love before, and now it only remained for him to find the right time to tell her how he felt. Now was not that time. Not while they were both basking in the afterglow of mind-blowing sex. He'd choose his time. Lucia meant the world to him, so he had to get it absolutely right.

They came out of the caravan arm in arm to find that it had somehow, mysteriously, moved several yards down the field.

'How could that have happened?' Lucia puzzled as she stared at the tracks.

'I can't imagine,' he murmured, tongue in cheek.

She looked at him blankly and then understood. 'You mean we—?'

'We'll have no bad language here,' he warned, drawing her close.

She laughed. 'You were right about the caravan not being able to withstand extreme conditions.'

'Which is why I want you to move into the guest house, where it's safer. Or there's always my suite at the Grand...'

How nice would that be? But all the more reason to continue with her plan to succeed on her own merits, Lucia concluded. Then she could book her *own* suite at the Grand and invite Luke over.

'Do you think Margaret knows about us?' Will it change things? she wondered.

Luke's answer was to pull her into his arms and stare into her eyes as he said, 'It's time to start trusting the people who love you, Lucia. You have to let people love you—and to do that you have to let them in.'

'Now you've made me feel selfish,' she said, seeing the other side of the coin clearly through Luke's eyes.

'Well, I'd never say *that* about you,' he said, pulling back to give her one of his looks. 'Awkward. Stubborn. Aggravating.'

'I get the picture,' she said.

Linking arms, they continued to chat as they stood outside the newly decorated guest house, and then Luke said, 'I've been telling your brothers how well you're doing, and that in future they should be calling *you* for advice.'

'Oh, great,' she said with a mock groan, smiling as Luke dragged her back into his arms again. 'If you think I'm going to take on the duties of agony aunt for a gang of over-sexed polo players... Tell them to write to Holly. She's the expert.'

But it felt good to know that Luke was acknowledging that the tables had turned, and that none of them would ever think she needed a knight in shining armour to ride to her rescue again. Although some knights were exempt from that rule, Lucia decided, as Luke brushed her lips with his.

'I'll e-mail them,' she murmured, knowing that if she didn't distract them both they would have to go back to the caravan and move it again.

'You do have something pretty big to share,' Luke agreed.

'Like…?'

'Like I love you,' Luke said, smiling against her mouth as she softly echoed his words.

CHAPTER FIFTEEN

Get a gag for polo-playing brothers

Okay, it seems sensible at this point to re-establish contact with my brothers. Not only is it sensible, there is no one I want to share my happiness with more. Plus, the sooner I lay down some ground rules the better, as I don't want them sharing embarrassing little snippets from my childhood with Luke—though I guess it's too late for that. He probably knows most of them anyway.

I'm going to start in order of age and work through. And we're talking age in terms of emotional development with regard to their sister, so that would be toddler to infant—Nacho through Ruiz.

Nacho—I hope this doesn't come as a shock to you, but life has come full circle for me here in Cornwall and Luke and I have fallen in love. Your blessing means everything to me. You mean everything to me. And if I haven't shown my love for you in the past, please forgive me. Yours, Lucia.

Lucia—I couldn't be happier. Horse saddled and waiting. Talk again soon—Nacho.

Diego—You are my inspiration. You have proved that however difficult you make it for someone to love you—and, boy, have you and I made it difficult—there are some stubborn people out there who can see something in us that no one else can. Luke sees something in me. Perhaps I should introduce him to Maxie? Seems they've both got what it takes to tame an Acosta.

Maxie here, babe. So thrilled for you. I *love* Luke. Will tell Diego as soon as he comes off the polo field. Let me know if there's anything I can do—anything at all...maybe plan a wedding?

Kruz—Don't start, okay? So you won't want to hear this, but it's about time you and I were back in touch, don't you think? I'm in love. With Luke. Luke Forster. And if you even *think* of telling him about the time when I ate dog food as a dare, you are *so* dead.

The Luke? Does that mean the Enforcer will be playing less polo? If Luke's still on Nero's team and playing against us, that can only be a good thing—no? Kruz.

Ruiz—No one pushed the boundaries more than you, so I wouldn't want you thinking it might be amusing to tell the man I love about the time I had to be hosed down from the roof after an argument with Nacho. Or the day I reported him to the police for confiscating my gum.

Sorry, Luce—you can guess where Ruiz is. Do you need the services of an agony aunt, or is that just me? Oops. Forgot. I *am* an agony aunt.
Love you, Luce. Whatever you want is what I want for you. And if I can do anything for you at any time you only have to ask. Xoxoxo

OKAY, so admittedly some of those responses weren't exactly what she had hoped for. It seemed the world went on turning and the only thing that had changed was how she and Luke felt about each other. Polo men were difficult, she thought, glancing at him.

Had anyone said this would be easy?

As their love affair progressed things moved fast towards the forthcoming party and the high-profile polo match on the beach. To draw the crowds Luke had arranged for several top international polo players to attend. He would head one team, while Lucia's notorious brother Nacho would head the other. Luke's parents were also expected to attend. The Fearsome Forsters, as Lucia had used to think of them when she was a child. Daddy Forster was a self-confessed stiff-backed son of old money, while Luke's mother was so posh she'd make a queen look common.

Wanting to make sure she had everything covered, Lucia had called a meeting in the cosy kitchen for a final chat-through.

'I'll leave you two to get on with things,' Margaret said when the meeting was over. She sensed love in the air, and Margaret's blue eyes were sparkling with suppressed excitement.

It seemed all her ghosts had been laid to rest, Lucia reflected as Luke reached for her hand. She had no worries about her brothers coming to Cornwall to spirit her back to Argentina, where she'd resume Cinderella duties at the ranch. Luke would never put up with it, and she had moved way past that.

Margaret stopped by the door on her way out of the room. 'There goes the old caravan,' she said, reminding them that Luke had arranged for brand-new lodges to be raised on proper foundations in the holiday park. 'I have fond memories of that caravan,' she mused as it trundled past the window.

Lucia hardly dared raise her eyes to Luke's.

If she had one worry now it was the thought of Luke's parents attending the party. Mr and Mrs Forster idolised their only son, and Lucia couldn't imagine that anyone would ever be good enough in their eyes for Luke.

As if sensing her concern, Luke put his arm around her shoulders. 'Stop worrying,' he said. 'You've got everything covered. It's going to be fine.'

Was it? Then why was she feeling a niggle of unease?

Later that day Luke was in the stables while Lucia was standing with Grace outside the guest house, waiting for the Argentinian polo circus to arrive. Grace was still working at the club, but now Lucia had left she felt guilty at leaving her friend behind. She hoped they could always be friends, and she'd thought this would be a great opportunity for Grace to meet the rest of Lucia's family, about whom Grace had heard so much.

'This is something no woman should miss,' Lucia confided wryly as the first vehicles driven by her brothers and their entourage crested the brow of the hill.

'You're not kidding!' Grace exclaimed as the parade of vehicles came closer. 'Who *is* that incredible-looking man?'

'Which one?' Lucia intoned in a mock-weary tone. She was used to fending off questions about her brothers.

'That big one with the wild black hair and tattoos.'

'I'm afraid you're going to have to be a little more specific...'

'And an earring. Oh, my goodness,' Grace breathed, clutching her chest. 'He's *totally* sex on legs.'

'I'm afraid I'm no closer,' Lucia admitted. 'I have four brothers, all with dark hair and tattoos, and at least a couple of them wear earrings. Brigands are in vogue this year, I'm told,' she added dryly.

'The one leaning out of the window of that black tank on

wheels.' Grace clutched her arm. 'Lucia—he's looking at me like he can see right through my clothes.'

'Nacho, you wretch!' Lucia exclaimed as the beast of an SUV slowed to a halt beside them. 'Do you have nothing better to do than terrorise my friends?'

'Just looking,' Nacho said without apology but with a wolfish smile. 'Nice friend...' And with one last appraisal Nacho pushed the sunglasses back up his nose and closed the window.

If only everything in life could go so as smoothly as this, Lucia thought later, hoping those would never be classed as 'famous last words' as she spotted Grace and Nacho chatting to each other in the yard.

Nacho towered over Grace, who was quite tall herself, and Lucia's typically taciturn brother seemed unusually animated today. With a smile she hurried on to make sure everything was ready inside the guest house for Luke's parents.

The Forsters arrived about an hour later, with an entourage of their own, and Lucia was hugely relieved when both Luke's father and mother declared themselves charmed by the guest house.

Well, that was two discerning families satisfied, she concluded, as Nacho added his praise to theirs.

'The Sundowner is even better than I remember,' Luke's mother was assuring Margaret. 'Always so quaint. And now *so* of the moment...'

Margaret looked blankly at Lucia.

'Thank you,' Lucia said brightly, stepping in.

'And Margaret tells me *you* were the driving force behind the restoration of the guest house?' Luke's mother commented, sizing Lucia up.

It was some time since they'd seen each other, Lucia reassured herself as she explained that putting the Sundowner back on the map had been a team effort. 'We all played our part,' she said pleasantly.

'With Luke's money...'

A million responses flashed through Lucia's head, but she countered the comment with a welcoming smile. 'Can I show you to your room, Mrs Forster? I'm sure you must be tired after your journey and keen to freshen up?'

Round one to the wild Acosta, Luke's amused eyes reassured Lucia. They both knew that at one time Lucia might have retaliated rather differently to his mother's not so veiled observation that Lucia might have been a pleasant enough fellow guest at the Sundowner all those years back, but that she was under suspicion in her new role as Luke's business partner.

'Lucia and Luke working together...' Luke's father murmured, hanging back to share an amused and kindly smile with Lucia. 'Do you two have anything else to tell me?'

'Like that we've stopped fighting?' Lucia suggested.

'I was thinking of something more interesting than that.'

'I'm sure you'll love the suite I've chosen for you,' Lucia said quickly. 'It has a marvellous view of the sea.'

'And you, my dear, are more diplomatic than you were as a child.'

Lucia flashed a glance at Luke on her way out of the room. She knew she would never fit the mould and be stamped 'Approved' when Luke's father barely approved of his own son, and Luke's mother didn't approve of anyone. But what Luke thought was the only thing that mattered, Lucia reassured herself as Luke's hand brushed her arm in a brief show of support as she left the room.

He had arranged everything to the second, so that nothing went wrong. He had the ring in his pocket and he was going to wait until the party on the beach was in full swing and no one would notice if he had a very special private moment with Lucia. The match had created an incredible buzz, which was still reverberating through the crowd. The night was warm, the moon was shining, and a top band was setting the mood with sexy South American music.

Now all he needed was Lucia, who had gone to change out of her work clothes so she could enjoy the party.

Margaret was going to mount the stage first to thank everyone for coming. Luke would speak next.

Once that was done he would find Lucia. Guessing romance had never figured very highly in Lucia's life—mainly because of her fear that her brothers would laugh at her—he wanted to do something special for her. Something that didn't involve her brothers looking over her shoulder.

Grace had helped her to choose a dress for the party, which had involved a lengthy shopping trip to the nearest town.

'Instead of hiding your voluptuous figure, you should celebrate it,' Grace had pronounced.

So instead of a dress with a yoke and enough material in the skirt for a second marquee, Lucia was wearing a red off-the-shoulder number that clung lovingly to every curve.

'You look sensational,' Grace breathed in awe when Lucia had finished her make-up. 'Your hair's glorious.'

'Luke's never seen me dressed in anything but dungarees, jeans or a suit,' she said, craning her neck to examine her rear view. *Or naked*, she silently amended.

'You look fabulous,' Grace assured her. 'You only have to see the way Luke looks at you to know that he thinks so too.'

'I just hope his mother doesn't think I look too tarty.'

'The only problem you've got is that his father's tongue will be dragging on the floor.' Grace stopped as they both glanced out of Lucia's bedroom window to see Lucia's brothers sauntering into the courtyard.

'When you grow up with that bunch it's enough to give any-one an inferiority complex,' Lucia explained wryly as Grace groaned softly at the sight of Nacho spearheading the group.

Lucia laughed. 'It's time to pick *your* tongue off the floor, I think.'

'You're right,' Grace agreed, turning away from the win-dow. 'We've got a party to go to.'

If only she hadn't overheard that conversation between Luke's parents as she passed their room she might have been able to face the evening with all the new-found confidence that restoring the guest house and being with Luke had given her. Well…it certainly explained the sense of doom that had been dogging her, Lucia accepted as Grace hurried on ahead.

'If only she weren't one of those wretched Acostas, Donald,' Luke's mother had been saying. 'They're such a wild bunch. It's hard enough coming to terms with the fact that Luke and Lucia are working together on this tiny project, but to have Luke tell you that he has fallen in *love* with her…'

There had been a pause here, doubtless for a shocked ex-pression.

'Why couldn't Luke pick a nice, refined girl from the coun-try club?'

Yes. Why couldn't he? Lucia had wondered, not waiting to hear Luke's father's reply.

From the reflection she caught sight of in the mirror as she passed the door to the Forsters' suite now, Luke's mother was, as always, immaculately groomed, while Lucia felt more of a mess than ever. She'd styled her hair hastily, and it was al-ready falling down. She worried again that her dress was too sexy—it certainly wasn't something she could imagine any of the girls from the country club wearing. For a moment she felt sick at the thought of seeing Luke again.

'Lucia.'

She glanced up to see Luke's father coming down the stairs.

'You go ahead,' she told Grace. Lucia was managing the guest house now. She could hardly turn and flee at the first sign of trouble. 'Is there anything you need?' she asked Luke's father with concern.

'The suite is perfection—just a word or two, if you have the time...?'

'I've always got time for you,' Lucia said, remembering that the formidable Forster papa had been a good friend of her equally formidable father.

'I just wanted you to know, Lucia, how pleased I am.'

'I'm so glad you like the room—'

'I'm just trying to say, in my clumsy way,' Luke's father interrupted, 'how pleased I am that you have brought Luke out of himself, reminding him of a time when he was truly happy. By doing that you have stopped him becoming obsessive about business. At least that's what I think—and what Margaret tells me. She says she's never seen either of you so happy.'

'Working together has been surprisingly good,' Lucia admitted carefully.

'There's more to life than work, Lucia,' Luke's father said gently, 'as I'm always telling my son. Margaret says you have been through the mill, but now you're smiling again.'

'It *has* helped being here,' she admitted.

'You can't shy away from your feelings here—even if they hurt like hell,' Donald Forster observed shrewdly.

Luke's father must be hurting too, Lucia realised as she watched his face grow sad. 'I know you and my father were very close.'

'He was one of my dearest friends,' Luke's father confirmed. 'And it isn't easy for a man to make a friend. But it must have been hard for you to begin with, coming back here, Lucia?'

'Cathartic too,' she admitted.

'For me also,' Donald Forster admitted quietly. 'Anyway,'

he said, bringing her back to the present, 'I know we Forsters must seem a bit lofty sometimes, but I just wanted you to know that I'm glad you and Luke have found each other again. There is a sort of symmetry to it, don't you think?'

Was that a declaration of acceptance? Lucia wondered. Or had Donald Forster heard her hurrying past the open door to his suite earlier? Something in those kindly eyes said he had. But would Luke's mother ever be reconciled when Lucia was patently not the kind of daughter-in-law she had in mind?

She was wrong for Luke, and wrong for his family, and the last thing Lucia wanted was to buy her happiness at the expense of anyone else's.

CHAPTER SIXTEEN

Get a non-polo playing man
It seems fate has other ideas.

I might be forgiven for wondering if there is any other type of man. Even Luke's father was mounted on one of the quieter ponies for a brief canter round the field. And Luke has always been The Only Man. Even at age four-teen, when I first wrote the list, I only added 'non-polo-playing' because Luke had less and less time for me. As polo took over his life Luke could only be bothered to shoot me threatening looks and gallop on. Threatening what? I used to wonder. Well, now I know. Oh, boy, do I know...

So that 'non-polo-playing man' will just have to find some other girl to woo, because I'm hooked on tail shots, tackle and flying hooves.

THE party had started without a hitch and was still going strong. He was so proud of Lucia. All she had needed was a chance to shine in her own right, away from the glare of her four domineering brothers. Even Lucia's sister-in-law Maxie, who was a bona fide party-planner, had made a point of coming up to him to say what a fabulous party Lucia had arranged.

His glance swept the beach, and then the lasers flashing on a stage where a rock band was in full swing. All age-groups were represented beneath banners proclaiming, 'THE SUNDOWNER'S BACK!' and Margaret was in the centre of the dance floor, dancing with the local farmer.

Luke patted the ring box in his pocket, just to check. Tonight was the pinnacle of the lifetime he had spent loving Lucia. He turned to see her picking her way down the cliff path with her shoes in her hand.

'Luke.'

She felt limp with fatigue when he took her in his arms. 'You must be tired,' he murmured, stroking her hair. 'Must you stay much longer?'

'Until the last person goes,' she said, lifting her chin.

'Has something upset you?' He was surprised by the detached note in her voice.

'Someone,' she said, moving back.

'Who?' he demanded frowning.

'Me,' she said, already heading for the rock pool.

Kneeling down by the edge of the water, she seemed oblivious to the fact that her pretty party dress was soaking up the brine. Swirling her fingers across the smooth surface, she shattered the ribbon of moonlight shimmering on the cool surface. 'What have you told your father about us?'

'That I love you and want us to be together when this project is finished.'

'And your mother? What does she think about it?'

'What does my mother have to do with it?' He frowned.

'Quite a lot, I would think,' she said, still refusing to look at him.

Doubt coursed through him. 'Don't you want us to be together?'

'Are you really serious about it, Luke?'

'Of course. Why shouldn't I be?' His frown deepened.

'I would have thought that was obvious.'

'Well, not to me it isn't. I only know that I love you and want to be with you.'

'You must know what your mother thinks of my family.'

He swore softly under his breath. 'I know my mother's secretly thrilled to be here,' he argued. 'Danger is forbidden at the country club, which makes it irresistible. Whatever she might say for effect, just being here is a great feather in my mother's cap—'

'Rubbing shoulders with my four dangerous brothers?' Lucia interrupted.

'With your very glamorous and intriguing brothers,' Luke corrected her. 'That's how my mother will see it, I'm sure. And, more importantly, how her friends at the country club will see it. They'll be green with envy, and she will revel in that fact—'

'And me?'

'You're the only woman I want, Lucia.'

'You're sure you wouldn't rather have some chic blonde from the country club?'

Dragging her into his arms, Luke cupped her face so she was forced to look at him. 'How can you have doubts when I adore you?'

'Because I overheard your mother saying something to your father...'

She said this in her usual frank way, but her eyes were swimming with tears of hurt, and his heart went out to her for all the things he had taken for granted and which Lucia, growing up in a family ruled by her brothers, had never known.

'If your mother was here to advise you, she would tell you that some mothers find it impossible to think of another woman in their son's life. It doesn't mean my mother likes you any less. It means she feels threatened by you. It's up to both of us to help her realise that my loving you doesn't change my love for her.'

'But will I ever fit in with your high-tone lifestyle?'

Luke laughed. 'I don't think you know *how* I live. And why would you want to "fit in", as you put it, when you're gloriously unique and everyone envies you your originality? And fit into *what*, Lucia? I have my own life. My own house—houses,' Luke admitted wryly. 'And I don't want you to *fit* into my life. You have your own life, and I would never try to cage you—though I must admit you are a little wild sometimes, and could certainly do with some taming.'

To prove the point he drew her close and they exchanged a look that set both their senses soaring.

'Not here...not now,' she murmured reluctantly.

'But later,' Luke promised. 'Nothing means more to me than you, Lucia. You can believe that, or you can believe something you overheard outside a door.'

'A door left conveniently open.'

'If my mother did go to such fiendish lengths to drive you away I'll take it as a measure of her love for me. And since when have you been so easily put off? Aren't I worth fighting for?' he demanded.

'Pistols for two—coffee for one?' she suggested, starting to smile again.

'I should think my mother would be only too happy to take you on at hairbrush-fencing.'

'Which reminds me,' she said, reaching up to lace her fingers through his hair, 'I still expect you to brush my hair, as promised when you bought me that beautiful hairbrush.'

'I'll add it to my already exhaustive agenda,' he promised, though he was more interested in kissing her right now. 'I must be mad,' he conceded when they finally parted. 'Perhaps my mother's right and I *should* beware of the wild Acostas—especially as you're the only woman I've been tempted to go shopping for. Everyone else—including my mother,' he admitted, 'gets something chosen with care, courtesy of my very considerate PA.' He reached in his pocket for the antique silver filigree ring box. 'But I bought *this* for you myself.'

'Two shopping trips? What's brought this on, Luke? Are you sickening for a fever?'

'I hope you like it,' he said.

'Luke, it's beautiful,' she gasped, stroking the finely worked box with her fingertip. 'You have to stop doing this.'

'But not yet,' he said. 'Well…aren't you going to open it?'

As understanding crept into her eyes he added, 'I'd live with you in that beat-up caravan, Lucia, and teach kids to ride if that's what it took for us to be together.'

'Luke—'

'Don't look for problems,' he said, meeting her gaze. 'Look at the ring and then tell me if you like it.'

He had grounds to be confident, and as Lucia opened the lid and gazed at the ring, and then at him, he thought the past, the present and the future rested in the look she gave him.

There was silence, and then the tears came. 'This was my mother's ring,' she breathed, staring at the pretty Victorian love band studded with seed pearls and diamonds.

Nacho had told him the story of Lucia's mother spotting the ring in a jeweller's store when she had been walking down the high street in the nearby town with Lucia's father. When she had commented on how pretty it was Lucia's father had bought it for her.

'I spoke to Nacho—obviously,' he told her. 'Nacho was your guardian while you were still a minor, so I felt it my duty to tell him about my intentions.'

'Your intentions?' Lucia was sure her whole world had just tipped on its axis. 'Luke, will you stop with the formal stuff for a moment? Are you proposing to me?'

'I might be,' he said, giving her one of his looks.

'Well, either you are or you aren't.'

Luke merely raised a brow.

'You can't joke about something like this, Luke.'

'Me? Joking? You demanding a serious approach? You're right, Lucia. What is the world coming to?'

'Stop it,' she said, but without much force. She couldn't get too het up when she could hardly breathe because her heart was beating so fast. 'You actually asked Nacho if you could marry me?'

'I did,' Luke confirmed.

She half expected thunderclaps to rend the air and a screeching Mrs Forster to make her entrance on a rocket-powered broomstick. But instead the waves lapped gently at their feet and Luke looked more certain than she had ever seen him—and Luke Forster was hardly noted for his indecision.

'I asked Nacho because that was the right thing to do, and I told my parents because I love them.'

'And they were...?'

'Relieved that I had finally found someone like you,' Luke cut in as Lucia frowned with concern. 'Someone real— someone with a bit of spark about her, as my father put it.'

'And your mother?'

'My mother couldn't wait to get on the phone to her friends.' Luke's lips tugged wickedly. 'According to my father they're the toast of the country club, and my mother's friends are green with envy, as I predicted. Are you pleased with the ring?' he added gently. 'I know your mother would want you to wear it.'

'She adored you,' Lucia murmured, feeling there was still some hidden power connecting her to her mother as she studied the ring. And as for Luke giving her the ring here on this beach, where they had shared so many happy memories— it was like a blessing on their future lives together. 'Luke Forster!' she exclaimed as Luke went down on one knee in front of her. 'Are you really doing what I think you're doing?'

'Either that or my legs have given way,' Luke said dryly. 'So, what's your answer, Lucia? Will you marry me?'

Lucia came to kneel on the damp sand in front of him and, leaning forward so their brows touched, she put her hands over his and said simply, 'I will.'

Luke kept his room at the Grand, while Lucia stayed at the guest house to help Margaret recruit more staff. They had decided that while Luke would run the family business and the charitable foundation they would form a joint venture company to handle their burgeoning interests in the hotel industry.

'Everything dovetails neatly,' Lucia told Luke as she showed him the schedule she'd drawn up to take them hectically towards Christmas and the wedding they were planning to hold at the *estancia* in Argentina.

'That's a pretty tight schedule, Mrs Luke Donald Forster the Third-to-be,' Luke observed.

'Don't you dare,' Lucia warned, flinging a cushion with deadly accuracy. 'I'm not having my rampaging polo player turning into a stuffed shirt.'

'Would you rather I took the shirt off?'

'Is that a serious question? More importantly, is there time?'

'Margaret's in town,' he growled, freeing the buttons on her blouse.

'How am I supposed to concentrate on work?'

'You're not. I'll do all the work.'

'What are you doing?' she protested breathlessly as he lifted her.

'If you don't know now...'

'And what if Margaret walks in?'

'She'll walk out again.'

Breath shot from Lucia's lungs as Luke positioned her quite expertly on the sofa. 'Are you taking advantage of me?'

'This is a guest house, isn't it? I'm looking for some old-style hospitality.'

'I'm not sure I can accommodate you at such short notice.' Luke laughed wickedly. 'Past experience says you can…'

EPILOGUE

ROCK! MAGAZINE REVIEWS OF THE YEAR,
by your roving reporter, Holly Acosta

ALL'S WELL THAT ENDS WELL
The rumours are true. The whirlwind romance between Lucia Acosta, one of the wild, untameable Acostas, and Luke Forster, scion of East Coast society, is to end in a fairytale wedding on an estancia the size of a small country, ruled over by deliciously dangerous men.

No one can accuse Luke Forster of not living up to his nickname on the polo field—the Enforcer has insisted that wedding invitations include the note: No muddy boots. No spurs. No curb bridles on spirited ponies. At least not in public!

Needless to say invitations to the wedding are highly sought-after, and with only Nacho and Kruz Acosta un-tamed, ladies, the race is on!

'THE *estancia* has never looked lovelier,' Lucia exclaimed as Luke drove between the wonderfully familiar gates before parking outside the sprawling house. It was the best time of year for the gardens, and the courtyard was a riot of colour. The dogs were snuffling around—a little older, but just as excited to see her—while contented cats snoozed the sunny day away beneath the shade of vine-covered canopies. 'It's the perfect season to get married.'

'Any time's good for me,' Luke observed beneath his breath. 'I couldn't care less if it's freezing cold so long as I can get you into a hot bed,' he added, holding Lucia's gaze as he lifted her down and swung her around before lowering her to the ground.

'I've always dreamed of getting married here to the man I love.' She sighed, adding with a cheeky smile, 'You're lucky I invited *you* along.'

'It wouldn't be much of a wedding night without me.' Luke gave her one of his dark looks. 'I'm going to leave you to it,' he said, as Nacho's housekeepers, Maria and Concepción, bustled out of the house to greet them.

'Let me guess,' Lucia said. 'Stables. Horses. Brothers.'

'But not necessarily in that order,' Luke agreed. 'See you at the wedding, Lucia.'

'Hey, wait.'

Dream on. This was all happening way too fast. Luke had told her he was going to stay in the *estancia* guest house until the wedding night, but she hadn't believed him. Luke knew exactly what he was doing, Lucia realised as he disappeared out of sight. Luke had demonstrated quite convincingly, on so many occasions, that delay increased pleasure, and now he was out to prove by just how much.

Lucia's friends had gathered to help her celebrate her marriage to Luke. Grace from the club was to be her chief bridesmaid. The girls had just laced Lucia into her wedding gown, and now Grace handed her the exquisite bridal bouquet, composed of white peonies, ivory roses and dainty cream orchids with a deeper, clotted cream centre, all set off by clusters of delicate lime-green Lady's Mantle, which had been the inspired suggestion of Luke's mother.

'Hello…? Can I come in?' Donald Forster poked his head around the door. 'I hope I'm not interrupting anything important?' he said, looking round. 'I had the word that you were almost ready.' He beamed at Lucia's friends.

'You know I've always got time for you,' she said, drawing her father-in-law-to-be into the room.

'You look beautiful,' Donald exclaimed when they had exchanged kisses on the cheek. 'My son's a very lucky man, and I hope you won't think it impertinent of me if I give you a token of his parents' love, to show how pleased we are that you're joining our family. You're making Luke happier than I have ever seen him,' he added, when Lucia's pleasure showed. 'It used to be all business and polo for Luke, but now he's encouraging me to ride out with him again. He even told his mother she looked lovely today. As if Luke has ever paused long enough to notice *that*. I don't know what you've done to him, Lucia, but whatever it is, long may it continue. Now…' Donald continued, delving into the breast pocket of his jacket. 'Every bride should have something old, something new, something borrowed and something blue—or so my wife tells me. So she took me shopping today.'

Lucia had to be careful not to smile at the expression on Donald Forster's face. He gave the impression that shopping was some mysterious rite most safely avoided by long stints on the golf course.

'We decided to buy you something new,' he went on. 'My wife said this gift will remind you how to deal with a wild polo-playing man. As if you need any help in that direction.'

Lucia could only stare in surprise at the small jewel case

'You'll have to get used to being spoiled, my dear. I don't expect you've had much of that since your parents died, but Luke's mother and I will take great pleasure in spoiling the daughter we never had.'

Lucia paused, and then flipped the catch. Her friends had gathered round to see, and after the gasps came laughter.

'You are the best parents-in-law a girl could have,' Lucia said, giving the girls a closer look at the perfectly formed miniature diamond spurs. 'Thank you. Thank you both so much,' she said, brushing a kiss against Donald's taut tanned cheek. 'I shall think of you every time I wear my spurs,' she promised him—though not every time she handled her wild polo-playing man, Lucia silently amended.

'You were worth the wait,' Luke assured Lucia as he freed the cravat from his neck. Flinging it onto a chair, he opened a couple of buttons at the neck of his shirt.

They were safe in the glorious bridal suite, where the floor was covered with fragrant rose petals, thanks to Maria and Concepción, egged on by Margaret. The evening party was still in full swing, and would carry on through the night... with or without their company. Without, being Luke's choice. Lucia's too.

'You're worth waiting for too,' Lucia managed unsteadily, her breath coming faster as she leaned back against the wall to survey her new husband. 'Are you going to take your jacket off and make yourself even more comfortable?'

'What about you?' Luke said, prowling closer.

'I asked first.' Reaching up, she checked the diamond spurs glittering in her hair. *Start as you mean to go on, Señora Forster*, she silently advised herself.

'It's nice to see my mother has retained her sense of humour,' Luke observed, his keen stare following Lucia's gesture.

'Everyone has a different recipe for a good relationship,' Lucia teased him, dodging out of reach when he tried to catch hold of her.

Luke's eyes narrowed as he closed her down. 'Are you avoiding me or luring me on?'

'Which do you think?' she said. 'Perhaps I like to be chased.'

She screamed as Luke boxed her in. Thankfully he was a lot faster than she was, and soon had her pinned securely against the wall.

'Hmm,' he murmured, plucking thc spurs out of her hair. Several hairpins followed, and Lucia's hair cascaded down past her waist in an inky-black cloud. 'You are seriously over-dressed for the type of hunting I've got in mind,' Luke observed in the stern voice she loved.

'Why don't you undress me?' she suggested.

Moving her hair aside, she turned to present the back of her securely laced gown, which Luke unthreaded, whipping each lace free of its confinement with the skill of a gaucho. She was trembling with anticipation by the time the cool silk pooled around her ankles.

'You're certainly dressed for the occasion now,' he re-marked.

She should be. The bridal gown had the most brilliant cor-set built in, so she was naked underneath—other than for the blue lace garter her bridesmaids had insisted she must wear.

'Aren't you supposed to take it off with your teeth?' she challenged, balancing her foot on the seat of a chair.

'If I must…'

The garter was duly removed.

'And now it's your turn,' she said.

Luke slid off his jacket.

'And now your shirt,' she said, settling down on the bed to watch him.

Tugging his shirt off, Luke tossed it aside.

'Undo your belt.' Her mouth was dry, Lucia realised. 'Pull

down your zipper. And now your shoes. Apologies…your cowboy boots.'

Luke kicked them off.

'*Off,*' she instructed, lazing back on the pillows as Luke toyed with the waistband of his boxers. 'Nice,' she murmured appreciatively.

'Anything else?' Luke's lips tugged wickedly as he slid them down.

'Not unless there's a teeny-weeny you hiding inside the most magnificent body suit I've ever seen.' Making a circular motion with her hand she encouraged Luke to turn around. 'Perfect sex-slave material… You're hired.'

'Come here,' Luke murmured, his amber eyes dark and watchful.

'*You* come here,' she argued, reclining on the bed.

Luke shook his head. 'The bed's for when you get tired.'

'And in the meantime…?'

'You'll have to come here if you want to find out…'

The space between them vibrated with sexual energy, encouraged by the deep bass notes of a samba throbbing from the dance floor below. Slipping off the bed, she padded across the rose petals, crushing them so that their scent rose in the erotically charged air.

'You've made me wait too long,' she complained, lifting her arms to rest her hands on Luke's shoulders.

'Not nearly long enough,' he argued, teasing her as he dropped kisses on her neck.

But she forgave him when, lifting her, Luke flexed his knees and took her firmly. She fell at once, calling out his name and clinging to him as he held her safe in his powerful arms while she bucked uncontrollably.

'Was that good?' he mocked against her mouth when she had quietened.

'When I can breathe again I'll tell you,' she gasped, but

Luke gave her no chance to recover, and nothing more to do other than lock her arms around his neck as he took her smoothly and rhythmically to the edge of pleasure and beyond—not once, but several times.

'Shall we take this to the bed?' he said finally.

'If you're tired,' she teased him.

'I'm not in the least bit tired,' Luke assured her. 'I was thinking of you.'

'Anywhere, any way, any time,' she whispered.

Hours later it was dawn, and the house was quiet when she told him her news. 'I'm going to have a baby,' she whispered.

Luke stirred, and then lifted himself on one elbow to stare down at her. 'How can you possibly know?' he said.

'I know—that's all.'

'And how long have you known?' he persisted.

'About five minutes. Didn't I tell you that all Cornishwomen have magic powers?'

'You're only half-Cornish,' Luke pointed out.

'And the half that's Cornish is my witchy self,' she said, smiling. 'We're going to have a little girl, and we're going to call her Demelza.'

Luke shook his head, murmuring to no one in particular, 'I can't pretend I didn't know what I was getting into.' But then his amber gaze darkened into concern. 'Are you sure, Lucia? I don't want you to be disappointed.'

'I won't be disappointed,' she said confidently. 'In nine months' time you'll be holding our child in your arms. I can already see her, Luke.'

'In your imagination,' Luke tempered patiently. 'And we all know about your imagination—don't we, Lucia?'

'I'm a changed woman,' she said. 'I'm merely stating a fact.'

'Remind me of that fact again in nine months' time,' Luke murmured, smiling as he reached for her. 'Any views on your brothers?' he teased her. 'It may have escaped your witchy notice, but only two are left unmarried—Nacho and Kruz.'

'I *do* have a view, as it happens,' she said, putting on a dreamy stare. 'Life is going to get a whole lot more exciting for all of us—especially Nacho.'

Luke scoffed. 'Now I *know* you're wrong. Nacho's a confirmed bachelor.'

'Is he?' Lucia said, as if she knew something different.

'Yes, he is,' Luke insisted. 'But let's get back to us. I've got unfinished plans for you…'

'I have plans for you,' she countered, mounting up. 'Now… Where are my spurs?'

* * * * *

& *A sneaky peek at next month...*

MODERN™

INTERNATIONAL AFFAIRS, SEDUCTION & PASSION GUARANTEED

My wish list for next month's titles...

In stores from 21st December 2012:

❏ Beholden to the Throne — Carol Marinelli

❏ Her Little White Lie — Maisey Yates

❏ The Incorrigible Playboy — Emma Darcy

❏ The Enigmatic Greek — Catherine George

In stores from 4th January 2013:

❏ The Petrelli Heir — Kim Lawrence

❏ Her Shameful Secret — Susanna Carr

❏ No Longer Forbidden? — Dani Collins

❏ The Night That Started It All — Anna Cleary

❏ The Secret Wedding Dress — Ally Blake

Available at WHSmith, Tesco, Asda, Eason, Amazon and Apple

Just can't wait?

Special Offers

Every month we put together collections and longer reads written by your favourite authors.

Here are some of next month's highlights— and don't miss our fabulous discount online!

On sale 21st December

On sale 4th January

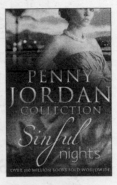

On sale 4th January

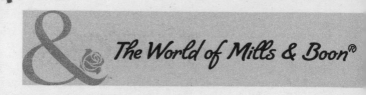

The World of Mills & Boon®

There's a Mills & Boon® series that's perfect for you. We publish ten series and, with new titles every month, you never have to wait long for your favourite to come along.

Blaze.
Scorching hot, sexy reads
4 new stories every month

By Request
Relive the romance with the best of the best
9 new stories every month

Cherish™
Romance to melt the heart every time
12 new stories every month

Desire™
Passionate and dramatic love stories
8 new stories every month

Visit us Online
Try something new with our Book Club offer
www.millsandboon.co.uk/freebookoffer

M&B/WORLD